Giovanna's 86 Circles

Library of American Fiction
The University of Wisconsin Press Fiction Series

Giovanna's 86 Circles

And Other Stories

Paola Corso

THE UNIVERSITY OF WISCONSIN PRESS
TERRACE BOOKS

The University of Wisconsin Press
1930 Monroe Street
Madison, Wisconsin 53711

www.wisc.edu/wisconsinpress/

3 Henrietta Street
London WC2E 8LU, England

1   3   5   4   2

Printed in the United States of America

Library of Congress Cataloging-in-Publication Data
Corso, Paola.
Giovanna's 86 circles : and other stories / Paola Corso.
     p.   cm. — (Library of American fiction)
     ISBN 0-299-21280-7 (cloth: alk. paper)
     1. Pennsylvania—Social life and customs—Fiction.
2. Italian American families—Fiction.   3. Italian American women—Fiction.
     4. Mothers and daughters—Fiction.   5. Catholic women—Fiction.
     I. Title: Giovanna's eighty-six circles.   II. Title.   III. Series.
          PS3603.O778G56   2005
          813′.6—dc22   2005005437

Terrace Books, a division of the University of Wisconsin Press,
takes its name from the Memorial Union Terrace, located
at the University of Wisconsin–Madison. Since its inception in 1907,
the Wisconsin Union has provided a venue for students, faculty, staff,
and alumni to debate art, music, politics, and the issues of the day.
It is a place where theater, music, drama, dance, outdoor activities, and
major speakers are made available to the campus and the community.
To learn more about the Union, visit www.union.wisc.edu.

In memory of my grandmothers

CARMELLA GERACI CALDERONE

and

ROSA TIGANI CORSO

and

for all the women in my family

before and after them

Contents

Acknowledgments

My thanks to the editors of the following publications in which these stories, some in earlier versions, first appeared: "Giovanna's 86 Circles" and "Unraveled" in *Italian Americana*, "Yesterday's News" in *Primavera*, "Freezer Burn" in *VIA: Voices in Italian Americana*, "Between the Sheets" in *Getting By: Narratives of Working Lives*, Bottom Dog Press, and "Raw Egg in Beer," *Not Black and White*, Plain View Press.

I am grateful to the Sherwood Anderson Foundation and to my agent, Evan Marshall, for their support.

My deepest gratitude to my in-house editor and husband, Michael Winks, and our son, Giona.

Giovanna's 86 Circles

Yesterday's News

Topaz, the thrift store clerk with the stickpin hair and rhinestone smile, shoos me into a dressing room as though she were swishing a fly out the window. With enough bracelets on her wrist to rival the rings of Saturn, she waves me in, pulls the curtain shut, and hands me the very same old clothing of my mother's that I donated to Yesterday's News weeks after she died.

I side zipper, suck stomach, top snap, suck stomach, double buckle, suck stomach, and back button my way in. The fit is unreal. It's as if the fat on my body is half-chilled Jell-O taking shape in a new mold. Even my reflection in the mirror is fooled.

"How's it going in there?" Topaz calls out from the counter where she lifts a pile of green-tag specials as quickly as the wind scoops up a bed of leaves. She stuffs the ball of clothing in a buggy to be re-tagged and circles back to the dressing room.

"Are you a different woman or what, Denise?" she chirps, her bracelets jingling as she puts her hands on her hips.

Up to that moment I had no idea. Before I stepped into this makeshift dressing room, I didn't even know who my mother was. Her life—outside of being my mother—was a mystery to me the same way mine, as a thirty-seven-year-old married woman who chose a career over children, was to her. I wanted to understand who she was before she died and I wanted her to understand me, but I never had the courage to talk to her about it. Maybe because I was afraid she wouldn't reveal herself to me. That I wouldn't know what to say, how to ask her and if I did, I wouldn't get the answers I was looking for. Then she suffered a stroke and never spoke again. I kept my finger on her lips as if it would help her form the words, somehow enable me to read them.

After my mother's funeral, my father, sister, and I cleaned out her belongings. I wanted to keep everything in the family because I knew how my mother labored over shopping. She couldn't just pick something out and toss it in her buggy. She had to inspect it first—seams, hem, buttonholes, zippers. She did this with all her clothes often finding imperfections even after they were purchased and brought home. In fact, the running joke was to ask her what she took back that day rather than what she bought. It was my mother's way of being able to participate in the ritual of shopping without having to spend money we didn't have.

Since my father didn't have a great deal of room, he didn't keep many of my mother's belongings. Neither did my sister, who lived in a trailer. Ever since I can remember, my mother pushed both of us to start filling a hope chest. I could never convince her that there'd be nobody for me to pass it on to. I kept a few of my mother's things; what everyone else in the family didn't want, I decided to donate.

So I drove up to a big thrift store bin in the South Side to drop off a half dozen bags of my mother's old clothing, but I couldn't bring myself to treat them as garbage. I suddenly got this urge to hand them to somebody. I parked the car, and once in the store placed the bags on the glass counter in the front and rang the bell for help.

The smell of cedar drifted through the air. Wrinkles on the garments seemed to disappear. Creases vanished. Clothes on racks rose up from their flattened state as if an invisible body were inside each one. Every top, bottom, overcoat, and undergarment floated on its hanger, defying gravity. Yet they all were evenly spaced, lined up like singers in a choir.

A sales clerk with a nametag that read "TOPAZ" appeared. (She later told me she was named after her mother's favorite Avon cream sachet.) Clearly, she was a company woman who dressed in company clothes, a walking testament to Yesterday's News: lemon boots and trumpet skirt; a red polka-dotted, ruffled blouse; and a crushed velvet, floppy hat.

I wondered if she was an illusionist, and clothes were the handkerchiefs she pulled out of her sleeve. The hat made her look taller. Gloves turned her skin into a soft, powdery shade. Ruffles along her neck were cascading waterfalls where she was bone dry.

"I'd like to make a donation."

Her reply shimmied up and down the well of her throat. "Great. You can leave them there. I'll take care of it in a jiffy." She noticed I didn't take my hands off the bags. "Would you like a receipt for tax purposes?"

"They were my mother's clothes. I don't even know what they're worth."

Her hand hovered over one of the bags. "May I?"

As soon as I backed away, Topaz untied the knot on one bag and began digging inside with her arm. "Feels good," she said, yanking out a short, olive green leather coat with crocheted sleeves and collar.

"I don't remember packing that."

"A car coat," Topaz said, explaining that it was what waist-length coats were called because when worn, it was easy to get into your automobile—you didn't have to tuck it under when you sat down. "It was a good coat to wear running errands in the Hudson Rambler. Like going to the doctor for a checkup to see if you were pregnant. Every woman was doing that in the '50s. They don't call it the baby boom for nothing."

I was curious. "How old is that jacket?"

She took a deep breath before she spoke. "Mid to late '50s. I'll stick my neck out and say '57."

5

"That's the year I was born."

"What's your name?"

"Denise."

"What did I tell you, Denise?"

Topaz was neon expressive. When she fished in the bag again, her flashing eyebrows told me she found something. "Ready for this?"

She pulled out a daffodil yellow, sleeveless silk top with darts that buttoned down the back, but I was still drawn to the jacket.

"No wonder back buttons went out of style," she said, wrestling with one to push it through its hole. "How's a person supposed to button all those biddy little things behind their back? 'Course, that's what husbands liked about 'em, you see. They could accuse their wives of taking forever to get dressed and needing help doing it, too. I'd have to button it up for you if you wanted to try it on. The dressing room's this way. Follow me, Denise."

"Oh, no. It's not my size."

"You'd be surprised."

"I couldn't," I insisted.

Topaz nodded. "When did your mother pass away, if you don't mind me asking?"

"Two months ago."

She gently patted the clothes she had pulled out of the bag. "Are you sure you don't want to keep some of these, Denise? They're vintage clothing. Right back in style," she said, adjusting the buckle on her yellow boot. "Look here."

She flipped the car coat inside out and showed me the lining. It was a peach print with white rabbits wearing tails, top hats, and canes. "Now it's the rabbit's turn to pull something out of the hat. That's real magic. You ought to hang on to this."

I smiled politely but that wasn't enough of an answer for Topaz. She said I might feel differently if I tried on some of my mother's clothing, and I told her the only thing that would prove was that my mother was more petite. She insisted size didn't matter.

An elderly woman in a solid blue shift knocked at the double doors. They were wide open, but Topaz excused herself and hurried over to greet her. The woman immediately wiped her feet as soon as she entered even though there was no doormat on the hardwood floor.

"You're a few minutes late today, Mary Alma," Topaz said, taking her umbrella and plastic rain hat to put behind the counter.

The woman shrugged her shoulders and excused herself in Italian, *"Mi scusi. Mi scusi."* She had salt and pepper hair and a single line running down the middle of her forehead like a crease on a pant leg.

Topaz held her hands and assured her. "You don't have to apologize to me, honey. Whenever you get here, you get here. You know you're welcome anytime."

The sun began to filter through the clothes on display by the windows, carrying their colors clear across the room like stained glass. It was suddenly so quiet that you could even hear a distant plane jet across the sky.

"Would you like to pick something out yourself today?" Topaz asked.

The woman shook her head. *"Destino."*

"I've got just the thing for you," Topaz said, reaching for my mother's car coat. "How's this?"

Before the woman had a chance to answer, Topaz took her arm and guided her to the dressing room. Mary Alma gripped the handle of her pocketbook with a fist-sized knot. She slumped so far inside her tent dress that I could swear she wasn't really in there. Her heavy eyes were nailed to the floor. Topaz handed her the coat and closed the curtain. When she returned to the counter, I asked her if she thought the woman was going to buy it.

"She never buys anything. She'll try on the car coat and sit with her hands folded on her lap in the dark for about fifteen minutes. Then she'll change back into her clothes and leave."

"She comes here just to sit in the fitting room?"

"Does it six days a week. She'd come on Sunday if we were open."

"Why?"

"Her husband won't tag along. He follows her to the market, to the laundry, to the shoemaker, to church, but he's too proud to come here, so it's the only time she gets to leave him, be somebody else besides his wife."

Topaz kept an eye on her watch. About fifteen minutes after Mary Alma went into the dressing room, she rang her bell.

"She likes when I do that. It reminds her of the altar boys," she explained.

Mary Alma emerged from the fitting room. Her purse swung from her open hand. The shift she wore somehow unveiled a figure. Her eyes were as round as buttons. The line down her forehead was gone. She sounded almost operatic as she sang a few words of praise to Topaz before handing back my mother's garment.

Topaz introduced us. "This is Denise, the daughter of the woman's coat you just tried on. Her mother passed away a couple of months ago."

Mary Alma took my hand and squeezed it so tight that I felt my knuckles rubbing against each other. She looked into my eyes as she made the sign of the cross with her rosary then kissed it before walking out the door.

I looked at Topaz, waiting for an explanation. "Come with me," she said.

I followed her through a narrow aisle, brushing against the clothes as if I were making my way through a crowded pew. I peeked inside the tiny fitting room and saw a gold cushioned chair with arm rests. An unframed mirror chipped at the corners hung from a rusty nail. She handed me the car coat, closed the curtain for me, and left.

The room was filled with silence. It was as though the pitch of darkness was slowly undressing my nerves. As I pressed my mother's flat and lifeless garment into the belly of my lap, I breathed the space between the walls, a distance that seemed to span the length of a gymnasium rather than a few feet. Oddly enough, this comforted me for only in that room did I find desolation equal to mine. I grasped the arms of the chair—long enough to feel its fleshy stuffing, strong enough to trace its frame of bone.

"Need any help?" Topaz called out.

I stood up and walked out of the room. "Thank you, but I can't do this right now." I handed her my mother's coat.

"Take all the time you need, Denise. There's no hurry."

"Thanks."

"When you're ready, they'll be here."

For the next week, I couldn't stop thinking about how Mary Alma looked after she had tried on my mother's car coat. I saw her serene face everywhere—through the shower curtain, in traffic lights, on my desk calendar at work—even with my eyes closed. I began to wonder if Mary Alma communicated with my mother, heard her say something she never expressed to me. Or if this woman had managed to talk to her the way I never could. I dismissed the idea as too absurd to even mention to my husband, so I started rummaging through photos of my mother, cards and letters she saved, notes she scribbled in scrapbooks, but found nothing. Maybe because I was looking for an easy way to connect with my mother like Mary Alma seemed to. I wanted to find the picture or the words that would explain everything for me, but knew I had to go back to the thrift store fitting room to find out for myself.

Topaz, was untangling a shoebox full of jewelry at the counter.

"I know what you're thinking. I didn't come here to buy back my mother's clothes."

"For heaven's sake, Denise, I'd give them to you," she said, freeing a string of pearls from a tarnished belt buckle.

"I was hoping maybe . . ."

"You're looking for the car coat with those magician bunnies. Am I right?"

"Is it still here?"

Topaz showed me the bags of my mother's clothing behind the counter. "Never left my sight. I had a feeling you'd be back." She whisked me inside the dressing room.

The walls are a pale yellow and the lined curtain blocks off the light except for a few fingers of sun that slip underneath, reaching across the wooden floor. She disappears outside the curtain somewhere. I find myself sitting in the chair, clutching my mother's clothes again. I am just as nervous as I was the first time and wish there was a noise or a shadow to distract me, but the only thing I see is the rusty nail. All I hear are Topaz' boots clicking. I'm in a holding tank with nothing but my thoughts. I feel the leather sliding on my knees and remember where I am and why I'm here.

After squeezing into a few things, I have the courage to try on the green car coat with the rabbit lining. It doesn't matter that it's tight. I'm my mother, Beverly DeMurio, and I'm behind the wheel of the family car.

My foot barely reaches the floor even though the seat is pushed all the way forward and my husband has put a wooden block on top of the pedal to elevate it for me. My hands are tingling from the cold metal steering wheel. My eyes follow the lipstick glare on the dashboard chrome in front of me. I'm driving back from the store where I had to pick up a bottle of milk for Nonna. I know she goes overboard pouring it into the cat's bowl. When I park the car and walk to the backyard, I find her sitting under the grapevine trellis, wearing an apron that flaps in the wind like butterfly wings and is splattered with bell pepper stains from canning all morning. Her long, gray hair is tied back in two braids. Before I can give her a hug, she jumps up, grabs me by the arm, and leads the way to the kitchen to make me my usual almond soda.

"Make that a double, Nonna."

She puts the soda glass down and grins.

"Yes, the doctor says I'm going to have a baby."

"It's about time you become a mother, Beverly," she cries, hugging me. "What were you waiting for?"

"I didn't know I could be this happy."

Are you a different woman or what, Denise?"

Topaz pats the dressing room curtain with her fingers, sending a ripple through it. When it stops, I realize what I've always wanted to say to my mother. There are other reasons besides my career why I chose not to be a mother. And one is that I loved being her daughter—I never wanted to give that up.

I get up from the chair, knocking my own clothes to the ground. I reach for the coat pockets. They are such small squares, but I fold my hands tightly into the lining's silky snugness and keep them there until I'm ready to leave the room. I push back the curtain to show Topaz the car coat.

"It fits," I gasp.

"You are a different woman! How about that?"

Topaz offers to wrap it up for me, but I want to keep the jacket on, wear it as I drive home, and imagine.

Between the Sheets

The morning low was ninety-two degrees, but the temperature in the hospital laundry room started to rise as soon as hot steam escaped from the open lids of washers faster than smoke out of a chimneystack. The steam spread when the wet loads were carried over to the dryers, and soon the laundry was floating in the middle of a cloud passing through.

It felt as though we were all playing a game of hide and seek. I saw little patches of the room but mostly just a hint of what was there—like Bonita, the girl in my tenth-grade gym class. I saw her looking down and knew she must have been reaching into the washer to pour detergent, but I saw only her brown eyes surrounded by a veil of steam like a bride before her husband lifts it up to kiss her. Or I saw just her hands as she folded pajama tops and bottoms. It seemed like she was pinching at the air over and over again. Everybody in the laundry room looked as if they were going through the motions, miming their jobs because the whiteness of the sheets and the pajamas and the bandages disappeared into puffs of steam. Even the industrial-sized washers and dryers hid behind mist.

The laundry room had no ceiling or floors, nothing ahead of me, and nothing behind. All I saw were the feet I stood on, laced up in my new Converses for gym class, and the cloud that kept passing through. I imagined I was in the heavens, standing on the wing of an airplane because of the jet-engine sound the washers and dryers made. I wanted to feel the breeze from being in flight, to fly away from the rows of dryers, each one a rotating circle of heat. As if one burning sun in this world wasn't enough.

Although I couldn't see, I knew exactly when Bonita took a load out of the dryers. I felt the current of air, lava-like molecules escaping with the momentum of a herd of elementary school kids stampeding through the doors to the playground when the recess bell rang. The dryers were so hot you couldn't touch the metal snaps on the clothing with bare hands unless you wanted to burn your fingertips. That's why, as hot as it was in the laundry room, Bonita wore garden gloves when she folded pajama tops.

By late morning, the temperature in the room broke 105 degrees. I wrapped my hair up in a tighter bun, changed into another cotton top, and pulled at the frayed edges of my hip-hugger jeans so they'd stop sticking to me. Still that didn't keep me from sweating where I never sweat before—in the backs of my knees, behind my ears, on my spine, in my belly button, between my toes, wherever skin met skin. And when my sweat began to drip, it felt as if bugs were crawling all over me. Everyone in the laundry carried hankies to wipe themselves off when they got too wet because our supervisor said she didn't want us dripping sweat on clean clothes.

The steam and heat combined sometimes took my breath away. I had to fight to get it back by inhaling as if I were diving underwater to the bottom of the deep end of a pool. I watched my waist expand and contract. I didn't like to breathe through my mouth in the laundry room because it made my throat so dry. I tried it once. It felt as if a cotton ball was stuck down there, and I couldn't swallow it. No matter how much water I drank, the cotton ball came back.

Just as I managed to suck in another breath, I thought I saw something strange happen. The color of the water in a washing machine with a load of sheets turned from a sudsy white to red. Pure red.

"Did you see that?" I asked my partner, Pina, short for Giuseppina, as we were about to feed a wet sheet into the rollers to be pressed. "What just happened to the sheets in the washer?"

I held back my corner of the sheet to point but had to let go as Pina put hers between the rollers, causing the sheet to come out with creases at the other end. She quickly grabbed it before it made its way to the folders who always reported wrinkled sheets to the supervisor.

I knew Pina was waiting for an explanation. I pointed to show her and said, "The sheets inside that washer over there. They turned red."

She glanced over. A cloud of steam had covered the washer, so she quickly reached into the bin between us and grabbed another sheet. I had to follow or else I'd leave her waiting with her back hunched over. I wanted to glance back at the washer but had to focus on picking up the same sheet Pina did, which wasn't easy since they all looked alike.

"The color of blood," I muttered. Of course, we were used to dirty sheets with blood or urine or hair clinging on them and the smell of someone's breath or body odor or disease. But it would never be enough to change the color of the water. I could tell by the way Pina was shaking the sheets that she wasn't in the mood to talk about blood. Her husband, Gus, was recovering from an operation on the third floor of the hospital, and that was serious enough.

So was our job. We shook the sheet hard enough to open it up but not jerk it out of each other's hands. Then we fed it into the pressing machine so it was perfectly centered, otherwise the sheet would crease at one end. The job required precision—not just for the sheets but for our hands. It wasn't unusual to see shakers with stumps instead of thumbs or disfigured fingers because they got them caught between the two giant rollers. Not only did shakers have to be fast to keep up with the loads, but they also had to have good concentration. So I had to try and forget about the bloody water.

As we fed sheets into the press, I pretended I was a lion tamer setting a crumb on the tongue of a hungry animal or a priest offering the host to nervous second graders who shut their mouths too soon on their First Communion even though they practiced for weeks with Necco wafers.

But my mind kept wandering back to the sheets washing in blood. I knew that pretty soon they'd be wheeled over to Pina and me to shake, only I'd be afraid to touch them. I remembered that when I was in fifth grade, my two best friends and I used a queen-size sheet to make our Halloween costume, a three-headed ghost. We were trick-or-treating for only a half hour before we stepped on the sheet and ripped it. We ran to my girlfriend's to put stockings over our heads so we could go back out and get more candy. Seeing disfigured faces inside the nylons was freakier than eyes in the holes of a boring sheet.

I changed my mind about sheets, though, once I started working in the hospital laundry where sheets started out as this wet ball of confusion in a bin—too much for one person to handle. It took two wills, four arms, and twenty fingers to neutralize the force of a single wet sheet. It was Pina and me against dead weight before we opened it up. We shook it back to life, out of its fetal ball.

A sheet was invisible when it took the shape of the surface it covered, a mirror, a bed, a body. In sleep you forgot it was there until the middle of the night when you turned over and your body went one way and it went another. You figure out that its skin is thicker than yours.

I was sure the sheets just wheeled over were the ones that changed color in the washer, but it was break time. Pina unwrapped the cloth around her forehead and the strips around her wrists. She wrung them out in the fountain and rinsed them in cold water. She practically took a sponge bath, washing her face, neck, chest, arms, and stomach with a washcloth before rinsing it in cold water again. I knew she was done when she set the washcloth on the back of her neck and wrapped the cloth around her forehead beneath springs of brown curly hair. The last thing she did was open a Thermos full of ice and fill her glass.

Pina was a lot faster than I was even though she had to be a good forty-five years older than me. But I kept up with her and couldn't imagine shaking sheets with anyone else. They'd just seem like slow-pokes. Plus she never let me forget that I had a lot to learn from her. Like when she picked up her glass and squeezed in some lemon juice and I said to her, "I bet you if you added sugar to that, you'd have lemonade."

"How else you make?" she asked. She looked at me and saw I was thinking hard about what I just said.

"I don't know. I never thought about it before."

"Your mom, she no make *limonata* on a hot day like today?"

"She buys Lemon Blend," I answered. "The same kind they sell at the swimming pool snack bar."

Pina reached for her pocketbook and pulled out a packet of sugar. She poured it in the glass, squeezed the rest of the lemon, and stirred quickly. Then she put it up to my mouth.

"Drink."

My tongue tingled from the sensation. "It tastes like real lemons."

"Miracolo!"

I took another sip of lemonade and sloshed the sweet and sour juice in my mouth as long as I could, wondering what else I didn't know because I hadn't taken the time to think. Some things I'd never figure out no matter how hard I thought about them, like the sheets. They were white and then red. Maybe that was a miracle too.

"Did you grow the lemon too?"

Pina said she didn't have a lemon tree here like in Italy, but she had almost everything else. She and her husband, Gus, turned their whole back yard into a garden.

"How did you do that?"

She mapped out her garden for me on a washing machine lid. On one end were the chicory, parsley, peppers, and eggplant. On another, pole beans, basil, and fig trees. In the middle were all Roma tomato and hot pepper plants.

"The fruit cellar is no more room," she explained. "My husband he cook and can all the way to the ceiling."

"That's what grandkids are for—to eat you out of house and home. That's what we do when we visit our grandparents."

"We no have children. I care for Gus. Help him with the fruit and the vegetables."

But she didn't expect Gus would be able to work anymore. Pina told me he was a diabetic now and had to get insulin shots every day. He was in the hospital because they had to amputate his leg.

Pina's tone suddenly changed. She asked me if we could shake faster to get through a bin early so she'd have more time to see Gus during her break.

"Pina, if I could shake these myself, you know I would."

She smiled, then we sped up the pace. We shook so fast, I didn't have time to look anywhere but my hands and the sheets. After staring at white so long, I began to see different shades that I had never noticed before. Paper white. Teeth white. Flour white. Communion Host white. All the way to the bottom of the bin. So much white, I forgot that after lunch, we'd be ready for the bin with the sheets washed in red water.

At lunch, Pina brought out a jar of Gus's peppers. She quickly forked one and spread it on a piece of bread.

She held it out for me. "You eat."

I already bit into my banana and peanut butter and was the kind of eater who had to finish one thing before I could move on to something else.

"Thanks. You eat it. Maybe when I'm finished, Pina."

She took a bite and said, "You always leave the food. I can feed the birds on the crust of you bread. *Mangia.*"

"I get full."

She poked my sandwich and said, "This no enough what you eat."

Pina closed the lid of the jar.

"Aren't you going to bring Gus some?"

"He no want food. He want the clean sheets. He say they no change for him. I say to him, 'Gus, we shake and shake fast. What more to do?' He no care. He want the clean sheet."

"Why don't they change them for him?"

"He say the nurse no like to roll him this way and roll him that way to make the change," she said.

Pina told me Gus said the next time they'll change the sheets under him is when he dies and they have to clear him and his sheets away to make room for somebody else. Then they'll put on clean sheets.

"And then?" I blurted out without thinking.

"God will forgive," she said as she made the sign of the cross. "He go to the heaven for the good Catholic."

The only thing I remembered learning about the kingdom of heaven were on old records the nuns played in Sunday school. They were scratchy and skipped a lot, so no matter what they said about heaven being a place of eternal peace, it sounded like hell to me. I didn't tell Pina that. Instead I told her about my grandmother.

"She's the most religious person there is. In all of Tarentum at least. Let me tell you, in every single coat pocket of hers, she has at least one rosary, two holy cards, and a safety pin with a string of holy medals. Even a scapula is folded up in there. It looks so old and worn, I bet it could be the same one from her Confirmation. Tissues stuffed in there too. But you know what else she puts inside? As if all that religious paraphernalia isn't enough, she throws in a buckeye."

"Buona fortuna," Pina said.

"Very good luck. I know. My gram gave me a buckeye. I lie awake in my bed in the middle of the night, and I rub it on its smooth side until the brown stays with me."

"You pray?"

"I hold it in my hand and wish on it and believe something can happen. I keep it under my pillow for when I need to feel something solid."

"You must believe," Pina said.

I got up and walked over to the cart filled with clean sheets and picked the whitest pair I could find when nobody was looking. I handed them to Pina and said, "Bring these to Gus."

She hesitated, then stuffed them in her purse before our supervisor approached us. She put her hand on Pina's shoulder and said softly, "Your husband would like you to be with him, Pina. Please don't worry about coming back to work. I'll have someone fill in for you."

Pina dropped the last bite of her pepper sandwich on her napkin and hurried out the door so fast the washcloth around her neck fell off. I ran after her with her pocketbook and the sheets inside. I caught up with her at the elevator and gave them to her. "Will he be all right?" She wouldn't look at me as the door closed in my face.

When I returned to the laundry room, my supervisor told me I'd be working with Bonita.

"Isn't Pina coming back?"

"I don't know. You can start off slow with Bonita, but pick it up."

Bonita was waiting for me at the sheet press. I looked down at the last bite of Gus's peppers and was ready to throw it out but ate it without thinking. It was juicy and tender enough to just melt in my mouth.

As I walked toward Bonita, it was hard to remember her in a tight gym uniform and pointy Keds that made her feet look narrow. Here she wore the same white blouse all the time and wide sandals that had to be two sizes too big. Even though I saw her every day at the dryers, I had no idea what it'd be like to work with her. I knew I wasn't going to be at my best since I was worried for Pina and was still wondering about the bin of sheets we were about to shake.

"I never did this before," she said.

"I'll show you."

"It's nothing like what I do at the dryers."

"Pina had to show me when I first started."

"You and her together look like one person doing it. I watch you."

"Her husband's real sick. I don't know when she's coming back."

"That's what they say."

"She's with him now."

"Sure she is. Every woman wants to be at her man's side when he's in that condition," she added.

"I'll go slow on account it's your first time. And you look a little pale. Are you feeling OK?"

"Don't you worry about me."

Since Bonita was closer to the washers than I was, I asked her if she saw the bloody water.

"You mean stains? I see my share of those."

"No. The whole sheet. And the water was red too."

She shook her head. "Nothing like that."

Bonita stretched her arm and reached into the bin without bending over. I took a quick look down. The sheets all looked white.

"My friends think sheets are boring because you shake the same ones over and over again."

"No more boring than pajamas."

I told Bonita what I wanted to tell my friends but didn't. "You know what I think? A sheet is everything to someone stuck in a hospital bed. Their world is flat. And square. Beyond that sheet is just atmosphere. A place they can't reach so it might as well be outer space. Besides, they're afraid of falling off. That's why doctors and nurses push patients smack in the center every time and then put the metal bars up. That's why a sheet wears out first in the middle because they all rest in the same spot no matter who they are. Everybody's afraid of falling off."

Bonita was impressed. "Wow! You know your sheets."

"Pina's the best shaker here. She can shake and talk at the same time when she wants to. Doesn't slow her down like it does us."

"How does she do it?" Bonita asked as she struggled to reach down for another sheet. I moved even slower than usual too, thinking each sheet was the one I'd seen in the washer.

"One day she told me everything about how she and Gus got married from the time they met to the time they marched up the aisle. She said his family knew hers and paired them up. Arranged for them both to go shopping down the Strip District on the same train from Tarentum if you can imagine. They didn't actually talk to each other until they got to Benkowitz's to buy fresh fish. She said

20

they found they had a lot in common. They both thought Benkowitz's crab cakes were worth the trip, even if Isaly's was just downstreet. Isaly's was mostly breadcrumbs and Benkowitz's was mostly crab. That was the difference. They both thought Isaly's made the best ham barbecues, though, and the best Klondikes too. Better than an Eskimo Pie any day of the week."

Bonita said she had a boyfriend. I figured I didn't know him because he went to Valley and we went to Highlands. We were rivals in basketball so fights always broke out in the parking lot after the game. She said he spends a lot of time on our side of the river, biking up Spring Hill Road.

"He's the one I've seen peddling up a steep hill with a heap of scrap metal in his basket?"

Bonita reached underneath the neck of her blouse and pulled out a round locket the size of a half dollar. "That's Donnie," she said, opening it to his picture.

"It's pretty. The locket, I mean."

"I was so upset when he gave it to me."

"Why?"

Bonita rolled her eyes. "'Cause when I opened it, there was a clump of curly red hair inside."

"You mean from an old girlfriend?"

"That's what I thought. But he said he got it at one of those second-hand stores, and the hair came with it. He just forgot to take it out before he gave it to me."

"Do you believe him?"

"He's a junk collector by trade and the second-hand store is on his route, so yes."

"How's come he's not in school?"

"He quit that. He's in business now. Full time."

"I don't know how he does it on a coaster bike. He must be in some kind of shape."

Bonita smiled. "He wears me out. Dances circles around me, girl."

"What do you mean?"

"You know. Doing it," she whispered. "He wants to marry me as soon as we make enough money."

The next time Bonita bent over, it looked like she was about to throw up. I asked her if she needed a nurse.

"Please. I don't want my supervisor to send me home. I need the money. The heat's just getting to me today. Understand?"

A new load was taken out of the washers, which made the place real steamy again. The thermometer said it was 110 degrees. No wonder it felt so hot. I made my way through the mist to get a drink at the fountain and fill a cup for Bonita. As I lifted my head from the running water, I began to feel light-headed myself and could barely make out Bonita. When I got closer, I could see she was leaning on the bin with her hand on her belly.

As we reached down for a sheet, I told her to just hold it while I shook extra hard, so it would open up on her side too.

"Hold on tight," I said, giving the sheet a tug.

It slipped out of Bonita's hand and opened up into the air, floating above our heads. I was ready to stop it from coming down on us because I knew it had to be the sheet that changed color in the washer. I looked up too quickly and got dizzy. My eyes lost their focus in the haze—as if what I was seeing was a dream. I felt something wet and saw the sheet already had covered Bonita. I pulled it back and thought I could make out a man with gray hair wearing pajamas and a tube in his nose. He only had one leg. It had to be Gus.

He was lying in bed with his eyes not quite closed because his top and bottom eyelashes didn't touch. Pina was right by his side. She held onto his hand tight like he was a child crossing a busy street. He grabbed at the sheet with his other hand, crumbling it in his fist. He kept telling Pina it was time for nurses to change the sheets. Call the nurses to make his bed over again. Pina told him not to worry. They'd come when he was ready. She watched as he slowly let go of his hold on the white cotton but not her hand. She tried to hold his other hand too. It was stiff, so she covered the hand that already held hers. They rested like that for a long time before Pina pulled the sheet over Gus, making all the imprints of his body disappear like a fossil buried in the sand. You couldn't even tell he only had one leg. She could pretend that underneath he was the man she met at Benkowitz's.

The room was still steamy, but I made out a nurse coming in to change the bed, and when she pulled the top sheet down, Bonita was lying there instead of Gus. They were the same sheets because I saw that the place where Gus had wrinkled it with his fist was now over Bonita's stomach. Her boyfriend was sitting in the chair instead of Pina, holding a baby barely big enough for two hands. Donnie, who was usually covered with soot, was cleaned up and even had his hair parted down the middle for the occasion. The nurse changed the sheets when Bonita got up to go to the bathroom. She brushed the bed a few times and patted the pillow before Bonita climbed back in.

I reached to pull the sheet down. Bonita was back in her work clothes, her hand on her forehead.

"This is the sheet you're going to have your baby on," I said.

"What baby?"

"You and Donnie are going to have a baby."

"How do you know?"

"And it's the same sheet Gus will die in."

"What's wrong with you, girl! The heat must be getting to you today. More than it is me."

She kept looking at me as we struggled to shake the next sheet. With each one, we got a little further behind. Another bin full of clean sheets from the washer was wheeled over to us just as a new batch of dirty ones from the wards arrived, waiting to go through the cycle.

Unraveled

Why Mrs. Natoli knitted in the cellar, poking away with those needles just to let it unravel was beyond me. When her knitting got as far as her lap, she started all over again with the same loopy yarn. Watching her rip it out was like seeing someone yanking a bandage off.

I stayed with Mrs. Natoli most days because she liked the company and my big sister, Lisa, didn't. Once when I was five, my mother made Lisa and her friend play Barbie dolls with me. No sooner did we open up our cases when they dangled a leopard mink stole in my face and told me I could have it if I left them alone. Before I could say anything, they pulled out a matching leopard purse, so I took them both and left. It was worth it because nobody around here carried a purse that matched just one outfit.

I haven't played Barbie dolls with Lisa since, and I'm ten now. The twins my age on our street are never home because they swim in the river all the time since you don't have to pay like you do at the swimming pool. So I can't play with them or my sister. Don't know anybody else except Mrs. Natoli next door, being we just moved here from across the river. Besides, Mrs. Natoli's cellar is like a cave that feels way inside. The door is so thick, you can't hear any outside noises, at least the kind I don't want to hear—the twins giggling on their way to the river every morning, rolling a gigantic inner tube. They take turns with it, relay style. I wish my mom heard the part about them sharing because then maybe she'd let me go with them. She's always telling me and Lisa that she can't afford to buy two of everything no more. Nobody can since they shut the mirror works down.

For the longest time, I figured Mrs. Natoli only knitted with one ball of yarn because nobody left the house to buy her more. She was a widow who lived with her daughter, Rosetta, and son-in-law, Harold. I knew for a fact G.C. Murphy's sold yarns and threads across from the goldfish, but nobody in the Natoli family got out much because none of them had work. Every day, Mrs. Natoli knitted in her cool, dark cellar until the ball got smaller and smaller like a bar of soap melting so slow you couldn't see it happening. Rosetta, who smelled of baby powder, was hoping to get pregnant. She rested on the couch with tea bags over her eyes and the radio on so low all you heard was static that made her knees jiggle.

Harold called himself a science teacher, but my sister said he was a milkman until he smashed the delivery truck. Anyway, he practiced his science lectures with goggles on in front of the bathroom mirror and made me his audience. With every word he spoke, I fixed my eyes on the dribble in the crack of his mouth, waiting for him to swallow or spit it out. He pretended there was a camera in the medicine chest to record his every word and move. He even shifted me to the side once when I stood in his way. Said I was in the camera's view.

Harold told jokes about lab safety when he lectured. His favorite one went like this: "If you burn yourself, remember do not put butter on it. Do you know why? Because your finger is not a piece of toast."

I was so sure Mrs. Natoli only had one ball of yarn, but when I snuck a peek in her knitting tin while she was getting me a glass of mint ginger ale, I saw at least five more of the same color blue—as pale as toothpaste. Then I thought she had to do everything just perfect and kept ripping out her rows until the edges were measuring-stick even. When I got a good look though, I noticed some rows were trampoline tight and some were as loose as the brown hairnet my mother wore to bed every night.

I thought it might help if I knew what her knitting was supposed to be. Trouble was, it never was big enough to tell, though it reminded me of a droopy tent about to collapse—the kind you pitch in the dark without a flashlight. I kept watching her blue ball of yarn spin slowly on the cement floor, a globe that was all ocean and no continents. Then Rosetta, her cheeks streaked with brown tea stains, came down and played some Dracula music on the organ. It was the same kind they blasted in church after Holy Communion to get you to bow your head. She held onto those notes for so long, they didn't go away even when she let up on the keys.

"You can stop knitting," she said, bumping the empty music stand.

"Oh, no, Rosetta. Not again," Mrs. Natoli said. She dropped the needles and yanked at the knitted yarn the way a sailor must pull at a rope on deck. She did this with her mouth open and her tongue drooping like a flag with no wind. By the time she finished, she had licked the pink lipstick clean off her lower lip. From then on, that's how I could tell she'd been unraveling.

My sister called me pasty face for spending so much time in Mrs. Natoli's cellar. Her smart mouth backfired, though, because my mom insisted Lisa take me to Sylvan Pool with her since we won passes in some raffle and they had a lifeguard on duty. When we got there, Lisa offered me her cocoa butter if I let her swim to the deep end with her boyfriend, Oakie. She dropped the tube on my towel and ran to the pool. All he did was try to dunk her and splash water everywhere. Lisa was always afraid I'd tell on her because as soon as my mom dropped us off, she took off her one-piece suit and put on the yellow string bikini she was supposed to have thrown out a long time ago. I never told because I knew the only sister I had would be mad at me forever if I did.

Still, my mom could catch on if she checked Lisa's tan marks. That's why Lisa never let my mother in her room unless she had a slip on. She had to cross her legs too to hide the scar she made on her thigh. A thick capital O for Oakie that was perfect enough to show Sister Virginia, my handwriting teacher, if she had used a ballpoint pen instead of a razor blade.

My sister wouldn't explain. Said I was a blabbermouth. The only secret she told me was about menstruation because when I asked my mother about it, she said to look it up in the big dictionary in my sister's room. Lisa said I'd have to wear a pad on my underwear to catch the blood. Then she explained the part about getting pregnant. I told her Rosetta next door wanted to stop menstruating and Lisa said Rosetta was never going to have her own baby.

"She wants one real bad."

"It doesn't work that way, Renata," Lisa said, getting close to the mirror to curl her eyelashes.

"Mrs. Natoli wants her to have one too. Just as bad."

"She can't," Lisa snapped. "There's something wrong with her."

"But Mrs. Natoli is always knitting. It must be for Rosetta."

Lisa pulled away from the mirror and looked at me. "She's wasting her time, Renata."

"Yeah, only because she rips it out," I said, waiting to see if Lisa would accidentally curl her lids instead of her lashes.

Now Lisa was applying mascara when she answered, "See. She knows."

"She starts over again though."

"She should stick to making hats and mittens," Lisa said, batting her eyelashes.

"It's not what she wants."

"I know that, Renata. I just mean she's good at it, that's all."

My mother had Mrs. Natoli knit my sister and me a hat and mitten set for Christmas. I loved mine. It was the only reason I liked winter at all. Lisa hated hers. She stuffed it in the back of her closet.

My mom always told her to bundle up every morning before she left for school. My sister would lift her collar and give her the tiniest kiss on the cheek before she walked out the door. I didn't say anything to my mother, but I knew she met up with Oakie down the street and they'd walk to school together.

The day my sister told me about menstruation, I went to Mrs. Natoli's house looking for pads in the bathroom closet to see if Rosetta was pregnant. Harold was rehearsing that same science lecture on osmosis. Each word was worse than a punch in the stomach.

"Osmosis comes from the Greek word *osmos,* which means the action of pushing," he said, signaling his hands the way a traffic cop does with white gloves on. "The action of pushing. The action of pushing. So what is osmosis? Why, it's the diffusion of fluid through a semipermeable membrane until there is an equal concentration of fluid on either side of the membrane. An equal concentration on either side. Either side." His big white lab coat filled the mirror.

"You mean it spreads like magic?"

"Not magic. Science," Harold said.

"It don't take no scientist to do what you're saying, Harold. It's the same as relay style."

He adjusted his goggles. "Let me explain it to . . ."

"Taking turns is the same as sharing," I interrupted. "Everyone around here needs to do that. You can't buy two of everything. That's what my mom thinks, anyway."

I began rooting under the sink for menstrual pads. I didn't see any and thought Rosetta must be pregnant. I stood up between Harold and the mirror and repeated the joke my sister told me.

"What's up tight, out of sight, and in the groove?"

"Cut," he snapped. "Not while I'm taping."

"Just guess if you don't know."

"Is there an equal concentration of fluid on both sides?"

"You're not even close, Harold."

"Is it on either side of the membrane?"

"You're so square. I'd give up if I were you."

He lifted his goggles. "You want me to give up?"

"A Kotex pad." I walked out to visit Rosetta upstairs and left Harold staring in the mirror with a wrinkled forehead.

"Harold's real scientific, isn't he?" I asked her.

"It's what he loves most."

"But what about you?"

"When I have a baby, I'll love it the most," she said, cupping both her elbows with her hands. "Did you know she's gonna look just like me?"

"You mean, like twins?"

"Just like twins," she answered. "We're going to be so close to each other, you won't know where one of us stops and the other begins."

She kept staring at her wrist as if it were the neck of a baby and her knuckles were the tips of its toes, singing pieces of different lullabies that she strung together.

"Mama's little baby loves, don't say a word, put on the skillet, bring out the butter, go to sleep my little baby, when you wake you shall have shortening, shortening, hush little baby, shortening bread."

I took the powder from the coffee table, sprinkled white puffs on her arms and rubbed until it crawled under her skin. I knew the smell would keep her company until she had a real baby.

After that, I ran across the street to tell my sister she was wrong about Rosetta. My father was home awful early from work. He put his lunch bucket down, and he and my mother sat on the living room couch we never used unless there's company.

"Leave your sister alone. She's grounded," my mother said as I went up the stairs.

I gently knocked on Lisa's door.

"What?" Lisa said in that tone my father hates.

"Shhh. I'm not supposed to be here."

"I don't care."

"Guess who's expecting? This time for real."

"What is this? Some kind of joke?"

"Lisa, I want to tell you something."

"Tell me what?"

"Rosetta's expecting," I whispered.

"She's not the only one who knows how to get pregnant. I didn't even do anything wrong."

"Maybe you did the same thing as Rosetta."

"She always miscarries."

"Are you afraid you'll lose yours?"

"I don't want a baby, Renata. I have three more years left of high school."

"What are you going to do?"

Lisa finally opened the door, and I tiptoed in. "Mom and Dad are sending me to Aunt Nancina's camp for the summer."

I sat down on the bed beside her. "You're going on vacation up the river when you're grounded?"

"It's not a vacation, Renata. I'm being punished."

"You'll get to go swimming, won't you?"

"No way. I'm sick to my stomach."

"So? Stomachaches go away, right?"

Lisa put her hands on her head. "By that time, I'll be too . . . it'll be too cold."

"You're going to stay there in the wintertime?"

"I'll be there for months, Renata."

"Then you'll make hot chocolate with marshmallows."

"I'm not thinking about that." She leaned back on a propped-up pillow.

"You can take my Nancy Drew mysteries. I have the whole set now."

"Wish they'd let me take my stereo. That's all I want."

I looked down and saw Lisa had her big suitcase opened up on the side of the bed but very few clothes in it. I guess she had to buy new ones that fit. I offered to take up knitting for her. Make the same thing Mrs. Natoli was for Rosetta except I wouldn't keep unraveling mine. Lisa said she wasn't worried. She'd take one of Oakie's sweatshirts.

"He said he'd come and visit me after."

"How come?"

She paused before she said in a broken voice, "He's afraid he'd want to keep it."

"Lisa? Open that door!" It was Mom.

Lisa sprung off her bed and slit the door open a crack. "What?"

"Tell him he's not to ever call here again or set foot near this house! Is that understood!?"

"Yes. I heard you." She walked over to me. "I have to pack some more."

"Already? But I want you to stay."

"I'm leaving this weekend. They can't wait to get rid of me before I start to show."

I slipped out of her room, and she slammed the door shut. I pulled out the cocoa butter Lisa gave me at Sylvan Pool and knocked again.

"I have something for you."

"The answer is no! I don't want to play swapsies with your clothes, Renata."

"It's not that. It's something else. I promise."

"What?"

I could tell by her voice that she was still far away from the door. "Please."

As soon as she opened the door, I slipped her the suntan lotion. "You'll use this more than I will." I prayed she'd take it so at least we shared something before she left.

"Thanks," she said, shutting the door so I couldn't work my way up to giving her a hug like I see the twins do sometimes. They hook their arms around each other's shoulder and walk with their feet in step—two right feet with red Keds and two left feet with red Keds. I showed my sister once and she said she wouldn't be caught dead doing the monkey walk.

"I bet you'd do it with Oakie if he asked."

"He wouldn't ask me to do that. He's not weird like you." Lisa would say.

I stood there, my eyes fuzzy. The wood on Lisa's door had no shine. It made my nose itch it was so dry. I began to wish Lisa hadn't taken the suntan lotion because I knew what would happen to it. She'd just bounce it on her mattress where it'd stay until she knocked it to the ground and then kicked it under the bed by accident. She could forget all about it and me. If I had that lotion in my hands now, I'd squeeze it out and smear it all over her door until it got good and greasy, until the doorknob was so slippery nobody would even try to go in to see her. Not even me.

I visited Mrs. Natoli the next day to see if Rosetta was as pregnant as my sister. She knew it was me even before I got there. Said my ting tongs slapped the gravel driveway, and everyone else's feet made a crunching noise. Because Mrs. Natoli's cellar was so dark, it always took my eyes a while to adjust, the way it does when you walk in late to a movie.

"Are you almost finished?"

She set her knitting down to get me a glass of mint ginger ale, which I especially loved when she took an ice cube, put it between a tea towel and cracked it with a spoon. Then I could have tiny chips floating in my glass like at the custard stand. She handed me my pop and picked up her knitting.

"I just started," she said.

"You start and stop a lot."

"I have to. I keep having to make it a different size."

"Who's it for?"

"My daughter."

"She's getting bigger, right?"

"We pray to God she does. She thinks she's pregnant and then she isn't. I keep hoping this is the last time I have to start this gown for her, but one minute she's blessed and the next she isn't. Each time, I say to myself, 'Guard your faith.' Then I go and picture my grandchild."

"Have you come close to finishing it?"

"I always have to rip it out and start over. Wouldn't you know, it takes no time at all to unravel."

"You're a fast knitter though, Mrs. Natoli. In fact, if what you do was the same as drawing a pistol, I'd pick you over John Wayne any day."

Mrs. Natoli didn't say anything, but her metal needles constantly made little noises like teeth chattering from nerves.

"Rosetta must really be expecting today."

"Doesn't matter what we expect though," Mrs. Natoli said, knitting with her eyes closed as if she were saying the rosary at the same time.

After she said that, I wondered if Rosetta was pregnant after all. Maybe my sister was right. It didn't seem fair, though, if what Rosetta wanted, she couldn't have, and what Lisa didn't want, she had to have. And no matter what, Mrs. Natoli hurried along her needles. I pictured her performing stunts the way a magician does so her knitting would suddenly appear or disappear. She'd sit on her rocking chair. Her assistants, Rosetta and Harold, would stand at either side. She'd start with easy stuff like knitting above her head and behind her back. Then Rosetta and Harold would blindfold her by putting her tea bags and his goggles on Mrs. Natoli's eyes. They'd hand her real big needles and real tiny ones. Rosetta and Harold would wheel in the clothes hamper from the bathroom, handcuff Mrs. Natoli and prop her knitting needles in her hands before stuffing her in the hamper. They'd spin it around and opened it after the organ music stopped. She'd wear a pair of polka-dotted mittens she knitted with the handcuffs still on.

Her last trick required complete silence. Rosetta and Harold would each hand her what seemed to be ordinary knitting needles, but in seconds her knitting would get so long it climbed up the chimney, covered the entire outside of the house the way ivy does, spread over the grass, spilled into the street like a flattened wave, and scaled our house. When it was completely covered by her knitted sack, Mrs. Natoli would put down her needles and take a bow.

I looked down at Mrs. Natoli's knitting still shaped like a tent sucked in by the wind. I tried to picture it bulging and big enough to fit two people, but that was too much of a stretch. I had this idea to fill a bucket with water and get Harold to splash Rosetta, but he knew right away I was asking him to do something unscientific. I figured if it worked for my sister when Oakie splashed her in the pool, and they didn't even want a baby, it could work for Harold and Rosetta.

"Here. Rosetta wants splashed," I said, handing him the bucket.

"I'm in the middle of an experiment," Harold said.

"This has already been tested. I know for a fact it works."

He grabbed the bucket and suggested I record how fast water evaporated when I placed it in the sunny window versus the one in the shade, with the window closed versus open, with the bucket covered versus uncovered. He even drew me a chart with the red pen he clipped on to his lab coat pocket. I threw his scientific piece of paper in the wastebasket and thought of my own experiment, relay style.

I ran back to my house and tried to rub my sister's stomach, which I managed to do because I said her Madras plaid blouse was wrinkled. I pretended to flatten it out for her.

"You can't have my shirt," she said.

"I'm trying to fix it for you."

"I don't want to play your stupid games, Renata."

"We'll take turns."

"Don't touch me."

I held my hand out. She slapped it down, but not before I patted her in the stomach.

"I don't want you wearing my clothes."

"It's not for me," I pleaded.

"I don't want you looking like me."

"That's because you don't know how to share, Lisa."

"Yes, I do. Just not with you."

I ran back to Mrs. Natoli's with my hand stinging from my sister's slap. Lisa's words stung worse, and if it weren't for me being in the middle of a relay, I would have thought enough about it to cry.

"Where's Rosetta?" I asked Mrs. Natoli.

She didn't take her eyes off her needles. "Resting on the couch. Why?"

"I have something for her."

"I'll give it to her."

"It's a surprise," I said as I went from the cellar to the living room. I found Rosetta asleep on the couch. She was white from the baby powder and her arm hugged one of the pillows. Her tea bags were all soggy as if she'd been crying. I pressed my hand on the middle of her stomach and held it there, figuring it would take a few minutes to pass through the pockets on her blouse, the handkerchiefs in her pockets, the thick elastic waistband on her pants, and the skinny one on her cotton panties before it reached her belly button.

I whispered in her ear: "The twins share all the time. My sister doesn't want to be twins with me. She doesn't know how to share, that's why. I've got to learn with someone. Might as well be you because you don't have anyone to share with either."

I went back to the basement. The cellar air smelled damp the way the sidewalk does the minute a few raindrops fall. The walls seemed to expand, making room for Mrs. Natoli's knitting. I swore I could hear them breathing but tried to tell myself it must have been the wind. There wasn't a breeze strong enough to budge a blade of grass outside. It made me think that something could grow in Mrs. Natoli's cellar. We just couldn't see it until it pushed through the cracks in the cement.

Harold went upstairs, and a few hours later, Rosetta came downstairs. She sat at the organ and began playing a song where her fingers looked like squirrels scampering across a telephone wire. It made Mrs. Natoli's toes tap. Mine too. Then she sang a lullaby, a loud one, and this time it made some sense.

"There's no trouble with twos, no trouble at all. You and me, we'll be mother and child, mother and child. As soon as can be, we'll be two. No trouble with twos, no trouble at all."

"It worked," I shouted, but nobody could hear me over Rosetta's voice.

I glanced over at Mrs. Natoli's knitting. It was the longest I'd ever seen it. She was three-quarters of the way done with a gown for Rosetta, and she hadn't ripped it out yet. Now her needles made the sound of two champagne glasses clinking for a toast.

"You're far along with your knitting. That means Rosetta must be expecting," I said.

"We're all expecting, Renata," she said in a cheerful voice.

Mrs. Natoli said she was about to start knitting the rows around the stomach. She said she would make them twice as wide as the other ones to make room for the baby. She leaned back in her chair. It's as if her eyebrows sat back and relaxed too. They weren't so bunched up anymore.

Then Mrs. Natoli did something she never did before. She opened the doors and let the sun in. My eyes darted through the blackness. I saw an old Victrola with the guts emptied out and filled with sheet music. A wad of blue wires flowed like veins along beams on the ceiling. Rosetta's organ, which pumped out music loud enough to circulate through the whole house, was curved and muscular. Angora hairs on a blanket grew long enough to run a comb through. Clothespins the same distance apart on a droopy line hung like discs on a spinal chord.

For the first time I didn't have to squint my eyes as I left Mrs. Natoli's cellar. Later that day, after supper, we drove Lisa to the bus station. For some reason, my mother sat in the backseat with me and my sister sat in the front with my father. It's almost as though my mother couldn't even trust Lisa in the car unless she could see what she was doing. I think she wanted a chance to find an apology on my sister's face without her knowing she was looking for one.

My sister didn't take her hand off the suitcase handle the whole car ride, and when we stopped, she lifted it up before my father could help. My mom got out of the car and kept her hands in the pockets of her pedal pushers the whole time. My father broke the silence.

"Take good care of yourself now," he said, stepping over to Lisa to give her a kiss on the cheek. "Say good-bye to your mother."

My mother didn't move. Lisa bobbed her head and kissed her on the ear, which was covered by the three-corner scarf my mom always wore the day before she gave herself a home permanent. My mom broke down crying and gave her a hug for as long as Lisa would let her.

"Call when you get there, you hear?"

My sister nodded and turned around toward the bus.

"Hey, what about me?" I shouted.

Lisa turned around and smiled. "I'm sorry. I forgot."

I grabbed my sister's hand and told her we could be pen pals.

Lisa hugged me with one hand and gripped the suitcase with the other.

"You write and I'll write you back," she said to me.

"Did you hear that, Mom? She's going to write me!" If she did that, I promised myself I wouldn't be mad at her anymore. Besides, this was something the twins would do anyway if they were separated from each other.

I wrote her my first letter as soon as we got home from the bus station. I told her the drive back was as quiet as the drive there. Dad suggested we stop for a root beer float at the custard stand, but Mom just took a sip of his. I ordered a single scoop of chocolate and a single scoop of vanilla just because I can never decide which one to get, they're both so good.

After that, I wrote every week, telling Lisa how long Mrs. Natoli's knitting had gotten. It was growing steadily. I knew because I checked every day. It practically covered Mrs. Natoli's knees and then began to drag on the floor it was so long. I used up most of my writing tablet explaining all this to Lisa when finally she wrote back and said she was about to have the baby.

I wrote her right away and told her everything in a letter—that when I visited Mrs. Natoli, she used up all the yarn in her tin and even had Harold break away from the camera to get her some more. He did when there was a commercial. Mrs. Natoli yelled to Rosetta to come down and try her gown on. She stepped up to a stool right through a strip of sunshine. Rosetta was covered in a web of blue that glowed so bright that I swore I could see right through her. Mrs. Natoli began tugging at the gown in places where it was too short. When she put her needles down to use both hands, the yarn dropped out of her lap and onto the cement floor. I reached to grab it for her, but it rolled out of my reach over to the cellar doors and up the stairs toward the backyard. At that point, Rosetta began spinning around like a ballerina, almost as though the force at the end of the yarn sent her in a thousand circles as the gown began to unravel. Her feet clawed the stool, her knees knocked, and her thighs shook like Jell-O salad. When the part around Rosetta's stomach was about to unravel, Mrs. Natoli pushed me out the door and yelled for me to stop it.

I followed the trail of blue yarn past the woodshed where it slipped between two leaves of wild rhubarb and into the brush. My feet twitched with every stone and buckeye that landed underneath my ting tongs. I could see the blue strip ahead of me except where it disappeared in the shadows of tulip trees. As I got closer to the river, the ground began to spring back from under my feet like sponge cake. Beads of moisture hung a pearl necklace on the weeds. The yarn was damp in places now.

I let it glide through my hand until I reached the end: the belly button of a baby. It was lying on a patch of green moss floating on the river. Its skin was as smooth as a clean blackboard. Its hair stuck to its scalp. Its hands made tight fists. A bubble peeked through its open lips. I never held a baby this young before but knew enough to hold its head. I ran as fast as I could and would have gotten lost in the woods if it weren't for the trail of blue yarn to follow back to Mrs. Natoli's cellar. I couldn't wait to hand Rosetta her baby in a nest of yarn. Finally, she'd have a baby to love as much as Harold did his science. Mrs. Natoli took a pair of scissors and snipped the yarn off the baby. Harold came out of the bathroom and took his goggles off. He couldn't wait to weigh and measure it.

Not long after I mailed the letter, I saw my sister on our front porch and rushed over to greet her. I asked her where her baby was, even though I was sure I already knew.

"What do you think I did? Let it float down the river? I gave it up for adoption," Lisa said as her eyes swelled up red.

"I thought you didn't want it."

"It still hurts, Renata. Oakie doesn't even care. He has a new girlfriend."

"I'm still here."

My sister nodded as her face broke out in tears, and I squeezed her as tight as she did me.

"Rosetta didn't miscarry this time, did she?"

I wanted to tell her how happy we made Rosetta, but it was too soon for that. I didn't know what to say to Lisa to make her stop crying, so I sat down with her on the glider. I was thinking of all kinds of things we could do together because we knew how to share now. She folded her legs up next to her stomach and locked her arms around them tight, so I pushed extra hard with the toes of my ting tongs, swinging for both of us until she let one leg dangle.

Nose Dive

I had just climbed into bed when a powdery black bird with onyx eyes emerged from the fireplace flue. Its wings in motion were slow and choppy as if it were the creature's first time in flight. Slipping on a robe and a pair of tennis shoes, I crawled out of bed, my untied laces dragging with each step. I propped the screen door open with a can of turpentine, grabbed the roller with the long handle that I had used to paint the apartment, and held it in my hand like a spear as I inched my way through the room in search of the bird. Its shadow had eclipsed the kitchen clock.

I crossed the French doors and saw that it had landed in a pot that was soaking in the sink. As soon as I stood out of its path, the bird made a swift exit, anointing the linoleum floor with drops of black water. The bird and its shadow were gone, and the walls were bare again.

My apartment was empty except for a bed, kitchen table, lamp with no shade, and the clock. I brought two suitcases when I moved to San Francisco, but I had yet to unpack them. The apartment felt no different than a hotel, and I never unpacked my suitcase when I stayed in a hotel. Rarely did I put my clothes in the empty particle-board drawers because I knew I'd be leaving. And the only way I'd unpack now was if someone made me want to stay.

Before I moved to this apartment, I had lived at a youth hostel in the YMCA at the Embarcadero downtown for a couple of weeks. Unbelievably cheap. Fifteen dollars a night and I discovered why. My window was so close to the freeway, it seemed as though I could stick my hands out and touch traffic. On a lumpy twin mattress, I watched as the big, boxy shadows engulfed the gray metal cabinet and then my bed before bulldozing through the cinder blocks behind me.

I thought again of the man I flew three thousand miles to be with. I was three thousand miles too late. He said it was good that I didn't stay with him until I found a place of my own. Better if we weren't lovers anymore. Best we not get in the habit of seeing each other, even as friends. Unless I got in touch with him—this from someone who blended up a Brandy Alexander after my first viewing of *Casablanca* on the big screen and wrote me a poem that didn't rhyme. He was the person who signed my organ donor card that same night because I was so sure he'd be with me when I died. He was the one who had me trudge nine thousand feet up a mountain to a rock jutting into the horizon just so he could tell me I was his best friend. Nothing separated us, not even the strand of hair blowing in my face that he brushed aside before we kissed.

After the bird flew away, I found a smudge where its wing left an imprint on the freshly painted wall the way a priest uses his thumb to smear ashes on a Catholic's forehead for Lent. When my landlady, Dorothy, came by the following day with a space heater, I told her that I had my first visitor.

"When? Who?"

"A bird flew in from the chimney last night. It frightened me there for a moment."

"You call that a visitor? You know what a wild bird inside the house is supposed to mean, don't you?"

"Bad luck. That's what my mother believed anyway. Not me," I insisted.

I explained to Dorothy that a sparrow accidentally flew into our game room once when I was growing up. After that, my mother blamed that bird for everything bad that happened in our house. She said it was the reason I charged into a wall in the hallway and dislocated two toes. She believed it was responsible for our porch roof caving in and for termites in the woodwork. My mother went as far as to say that the bird was the reason our new wall-to-wall carpet had to be lifted and replaced three times because the color had faded. I told Dorothy that no matter what vibrant shade it started out, each carpet ended up looking as if every drop of dye was sucked out of it.

She was eager to change the subject. "What happened to that nature club you said you were going to join?"

"It disbanded. The leader of the group moved to Alaska. I have to find another one."

"How about work? Anybody there you can meet?" she asked, setting the space heater on the kitchen table before she plopped onto the sofa.

"Nobody my age."

"Why don't you come to my son's birthday party? He has a lot of nice friends," she said, dipping her head so she didn't look at me through her bifocals.

Dorothy felt sorry for me because the young woman renting her garden apartment was always getting dates. Marija was never home and when she was, she wasn't alone. She was throwing parties, serving romantic dinners, or getting flowers delivered and gifts in the mail. The one time Dorothy brought me a package, she couldn't wait for me to open it—so sure it was a box of chocolates. It was the *Dinner for One* cookbook I had ordered.

"Dorothy, I'm going to have more company. More birds."

"That won't happen again."

I put water on for coffee and found one of the bird's tiny feathers in the sink. It was caked with soot and ashes, but once I dipped it in water, it turned a mossy green—so delicate and beguiling that I kept it in a glass on the counter.

"Don't tell me you think that means good luck?" Dorothy's tone answered her own question. "You're not going to sit back and wait for them all to flock here, I hope."

"I did that growing up," I said. "We had a concrete birdbath my grandfather made as a wedding present for my parents. It was so heavy that it had to go in the back of my uncle's truck when we moved to another house. One of my yard duties was to fill the tub for the birds while I watered the hens and chicks around it. After we finished our lawn work, my mom would bring out a pitcher of iced tea. We'd sit on the porch glider and watch the birds. My mom didn't mind them as long as they didn't fly too close to the house."

"Not to mention in the house," Dorothy added as she got up to put an extra spoon of instant coffee in her cup.

"Right. They splashed and fussed in the water so much, our neighbors across the street, the Kellys, pulled up two chairs and joined us. As if it were a movie, we all faced the birdbath. The Kellys always said they were going to buy one for their yard but never could decide where to put it. Mrs. Kelly wanted it in the front and her husband wanted it in the back. My mom told them how heavy ours was and once it was in the ground, they wouldn't want to have to move it again. I think they decided it was easier to lug over a couple of six packs and carry back empty bottles."

"After Mr. Kelly had a few, he serenaded the birds."

"I thought it was supposed to be the other way around." Dorothy gulped the last of her coffee and got up to rinse her mug.

"Maybe so, but we all found it amusing except for the preacher next door who complained we were making too much noise. Mr. Kelly told him there was nothing that could cleanse the soul more on this entire earth than watching a bird take a bath."

"Bet he never cleaned the bird droppings," Dorothy grumbled.

She still wasn't convinced, but I was. I put the wet feather and the ashes in a jar. I had this feeling I'd take them out the same time I'd unpack the clothes in my suitcase.

The next day at work, I took a walk in a nearby park during my lunch hour, my mind set on bird watching. I sat on a bench gazing at eucalyptus trees so dense in the sky it looked as though the branches were holding hands. A few yards toward the bay, the footpath ended and so did the forest. The soil turned to marsh spiked with reed grass brown at the tips so that I could hear the dryness rattle in the wind. The low waterline exposed soil with thousands of tiny cracks the way porcelain has hairline fractures. The clipped, amber ridge in the distance reminded me of the back of a leopard. Even the air smelled like every drop of sweetness was squeezed out of it.

At the end of the footpath was a young woman hiding inside a dark tailored suit that clung to her tiny waist, stiff stockings with seams in the back, and big octagonal glasses. She had the facial expression of a mannequin until she became hypnotized by what appeared to be a flock of birds, each one performing an aerial display. The birds took turns nose diving. Just when their tiny bodies were inches from the ground, they swooped back up in line only to repeat the acrobatic movement.

She flipped up her glasses, clutched her hands together, and gazed with a smile that accentuated her high cheekbones. Suddenly, she brightened up like a rock in water whose colors shimmered in the wet glow. I didn't know whether to stare at her or the birds.

"They're all doing the same thing, " I said when I finally looked up in the air.

After a lull of silence she said, "There's only one."

I quickly pulled a sandwich out of my bag and said, "How can it get from down here to up there so quickly? There has to be more than one."

"It's a mating pattern. The male persuades the female not to leave by showing off. He even positions his dive so his body faces the sun and his feathers sparkle."

"So it's going in circles?" I squeezed my sandwich so hard that a piece of avocado slid out and landed on my lap.

"Around and around for love."

"And the female falls for it?"

"Maybe it's got something to do with maternal instinct."

"Not for all birds. I thought I read in a magazine once while waiting in the dentist's office that a female penguin lays an egg and bails. Straight to Club Med for a swim. I mean, I'm not so sure I want to be a mother. And have a daughter like me?"

She sat down beside me and sipped her soup, holding the cup close to her mouth so her chopsticks didn't have far to travel. She told me this was the secret to using them—people dropped food because they left their bowls down on the table.

I knew more about eating with chopsticks than I knew about Kio, except that she and I worked for the same trade association and that I could watch her do anything when she was eyeing hummingbirds—even fidget the way she did, loosening the scarf around her neck, tugging at the cuff of her sleeve, centering the belt around her waist. When she flicked back her wrist and exposed the palm of her hand, her open fingers fluttering, she bore her soul to me. She didn't know it, but I was certain I'd do the same for her.

"Have you ever seen a hummingbird before?" she asked.

"I love to bird watch, but I've never seen anything like this," I said, my hands popping up from my lap like two pieces of toast. "In fact a bird flew in my apartment the other night by accident."

"What kind?"

"I couldn't tell. It was covered in soot and ash from the fireplace. All I know is that it was huge."

"Then it wasn't a hummingbird." Kio explained that hummers are so tiny their straw-like beaks are nearly as long as their bodies. They can fly forward, backwards, and sideways so quickly they disappear into the air.

"Can they reappear too?"

"They can do everything except soar."

Kio told me she had been watching the hummingbirds since she started working with the trade association a year ago. I told her I had just moved to San Francisco from Pittsburgh.

"I used to watch the rivers at Point State Park during my lunch breaks. It was a haven for birds." I told Kio how I'd sit as close to the edge as I could of the triangular strip of land where the Mononga-hela River on one side and the Allegheny on the other met to form the Ohio, a view of the exact point where the rivers merged. I could see the assembly-line rhythm of the Mon with its continuous stream of ripples from the barges chugging up and down the river. The Al-legheny was still and then all of a sudden a recreational motorboat would send the waters in to a chopping frenzy. "The only way I could tell where the Ohio began was by watching the birds. They al-ways hovered directly above . . ."

"The confluence." Kio finished my sentence.

"I never saw a hummingbird at the Point, though."

Kio continued to explain that they thrive on liquid, but like it sweet. They put their beaks in trumpet flowers to draw nectar. "Al-ways thirsty," she said, getting up to throw her empty cup into the trash.

I walked back with Kio to her office. It was a small room with two desks facing each other. Her boss, Heinrich, was waiting for her. He slicked his spaghetti strands over his bald spot and put on his suit coat. He was about to take off for a hearing. Kio asked him if he had all the paperwork as she went into the closet and grabbed a different color form from every pile to hand to him. And one more thing. She flattened his lapel before he walked out, clicking his heels down the corridor.

I asked her if she wanted to have lunch tomorrow in the park.

"If the hummers are there, I'll be there," she said.

That day, I decided to attract hummingbirds outside of my apartment window. I found myself excited at the thought that the sound of their wings, their constant movement and flashes of color would make me feel as if I were on a lively dance floor where secrets were whispered and the air was warm from body heat, where glances merged and thoughts rose to the surface of your skin and bubbled over.

After work, I went to the hardware store to buy a birdbath, but the clerk sold me a special feeder for hummingbirds that he said was guaranteed to attract them. I measured four parts water and one part sugar and whipped it in the blender until the smell of electricity filled the air. As I was about to hang the feeder, Dorothy stopped by.

"After yesterday, I thought you had enough of birds," she said.

"A question for you, Dorothy. Do you think this window has the most sun or the one over there? Hummingbird feathers are brilliant in the light."

"The window above the table. I wish you'd do something to get out of the house," she added. "We need a stand-in for one of the girls. How's about bowling tonight? It's a coed league, you know."

I scooted to the front window by my bed. "But this one has a better view."

To the north was the Transamerica Building with its pointy roof poking the sky. Fog softened it—gave it the mystic air of an Egyptian pyramid floating on a bed of fluffy pillows. To the east was the Bay and a faint sound of a foghorn dissolving in the mist. Below was a lemon tree in my neighbor's yard. He often walked to the far end of the tree with a bucket, dodging the fruit that had fallen randomly on the ground.

"Think I should get another feeder and put one outside of both windows?"

Dorothy frowned. "You should spend as much time trying to trap a man in here."

"I saw my first hummer today. They're unbelievable! I met a woman at work who knows everything about them. I'd like to invite her over to bird watch with me."

That didn't stop Dorothy from inviting me to her card club next week to play bridge. I told her the last time I played cards was Old Maid fifteen years ago.

"And don't say anything. I'm only twenty-three years old. I have plenty of time before I'm an old maid!"

A week later, I was still waiting for hummers, but none had come to the feeder. Each day, I added a new glass of sugar water, thinking one more would do it. I went to the library and took out all the books there were on hummingbirds. One book suggested hanging a fuchsia plant near the feeder because hummers are attracted to red flowers. Not only did I hang a fuchsia, but I put just about everything I could find that was red on the windowsill—red socks, red marimbas, red pens, red needle-nose pliers, a red shower cap, red oven tongs.

I imagined waking up beside a hummingbird flickering in the sunlight. Its color would be so brilliant that I'd make it out against the backdrop of red-tinned roofs. I'd prop my pillow against the headboard to listen for the gurgling sound a straw makes when a glass is empty and hurry to bring out a refill. It'd be a regular soda fountain like the Tarentum Confectionery. As a young girl, I remember spinning on a red stool at the counter until my mother said I was making her dizzy. While my sister and I waited for our cherry pop, my Aunt Mary gave us each a napkin with a thin, pink mint she slipped in from the candy counter out front. When she had time, she'd take us upstairs where the candy was made. My sister told me they kept a bird up there that laid all the chocolate Easter eggs. When I asked where, she pointed to an upside-down straw hat on the shelf that she said was the bird's nest and I believed her.

Another week passed and still no hummers. It didn't help that the weather turned even cooler. I stopped by Kio's office and asked her to come to my apartment, see the feeder, and give me some more pointers.

"It's too soon. Wait until it rains. They'll be back." She explained that hummers hibernate during cold snaps when the flowers close up. Rather than burn off energy looking for nectar, they find a warm soft place to sleep it off.

I invited her to go for a drink after work, but she folded a few papers on her desk and changed the subject. So I changed it back to hummingbirds and asked if I could tell her a dream I had after reading a Mayan legend of how hummingbirds came to be. She eagerly cleared a pile of papers from a chair for me to sit down.

"A peasant gathering wild berries in the forest saw a flurry of feathers blowing in the wind. She put . . ."

"Wait," Kio took off her glasses and closed her eyes. "Now."

"She put her basket down and plucked them from the air one by one until she had more than a handful. She sat on a rock to examine them and spotted a beak lying lost on the ground like a brittle twig snapped from the mother branch. She looked farther and discovered bones sprinkled about, a disjointed spine along the trial. She tossed the scraps in her basket, covered them with a cloth, and continued to pick nuts and berries. Once her basket was full, she returned home and tipped it over on the table. The mound of berries spilled out, but she noticed something moving underneath the cloth. She unfolded it, revealing an awkward-looking bird inside. There were no eggshells. No residue of birth."

I paused. Kio smiled and said, "Go on."

"The hummingbird looked to its maker for food. The peasant said, 'I have no crumbs. I used all the scraps I had to make you.'"

"'How will I feed myself,' the hummer asked."

"'With your beak, you can draw nectar from long and narrow trumpet flowers the other birds leave behind because they can't reach them.'"

"'Can I fly?'"

"'Your wings will be so strong, you can fly in and out of a crocodile's mouth so fast, you could make a meal on the food clinging to its teeth before the reptile could make a meal on you.'"

"'What color am I?'"

"'Gray. But since you don't have a colorful tail or true pigment like other birds, you can borrow a ray of light to reflect on each feather tip. Your iridescent feathers will flicker like a flame inhaling and exhaling the sun's fire breath. But when your back is to the sun, your feathers will darken like fire turning to ash.'"

I leaned forward in my chair to see if Kio had fallen asleep.

"Fire turning to ash," she repeated. "I'm listening."

"The hummer asked one more question: 'Can I chirp like the other birds?'"

"'You have no song, hummingbird, but we'll ask the air passing through your feathers to play a humming tune.'"

"'Everything I have is borrowed.'"

"'But you are as fast as the crane, as melodious as any song bird, and as brilliant as a Quetzal bird's tail,' the peasant said as she gesticulated dramatically."

"The hummingbird thanked the peasant, who replied, 'You are indebted to the wind and sun and flowers for your beauty and strength.'"

I paused and then whispered, "I see beauty and strength."

Kio's eyes began to twitch as if she were trying hard to keep them closed.

"In honor of the peasant's deed, the hummingbird promised her that it would always build its nests from scraps it found in the forest."

After a long silence, Kio spoke, her eyes still closed: "Is that your story?"

"No. My story is that you are the only person I can tell my dreams to."

She opened her eyes and looked at me a few seconds before putting on her glasses. "If I had dreams, I'd tell you mine. But all I have are secrets," she said.

"That's not true. I've seen you dream every time you look at a hummingbird."

"Let me know when you get any birds." She picked up the phone and waited for me to leave before she dialed the last few digits.

I knew Kio needed her distance, but I kept asking her to go out for a drink after work so I could tell her more of my dreams. She was always working late with her boss, Heinrich. She probably had a lover. Probably him. But then she'd say she'd come to my apartment if I got hummers. Maybe she didn't drink. Whatever it was didn't matter as much as that day when Kio and I watched the hummers together on the park bench and she managed to escape through her smile. Every time I remembered that, I thought of taking my clothes out of the suitcase. Then I could see her eyebrows drop and her lips close up when the birds flew away. It was as though she zipped herself up in a costume, and I waited for the day when she would molt her feathers. There's nothing as tender as a bird's skin exposed, the tiny blue veins and fine lines. Kio was hiding herself the way a child does when she squeezed something in her fist and put both hands behind her back so you had to guess which hand would turn up the surprise. And when you guessed right, she switched it so she could open up an empty fist. After a certain point, I didn't care what was inside. I just wanted to see her for who she was.

Each month that I didn't unpack, Dorothy was convinced it would be my last in San Francisco. I began to wonder too. Until spring.

It was drizzling outside, a gentle tap on the shoulder for everything to wake up. The hills that were amber turf, the texture of brush burn, were green and furry. The soil was smooth and pasty from all the moisture. Flowers were capped with color. And the hummingbirds arose from their torpor.

I paused at the footpath in the park near our office, inhaling breaths of eucalyptus in the air. Kio appeared at the park entrance.

"You and I seem to be the only ones who know about this place," I said.

"We must be the only bird watchers."

"The hummers are back."

"The flowers are in bloom," Kio said.

"I spotted a hummer's nest. Want to see it?"

I led Kio to a tree behind the park bench. The nest was a perfect extension of the branch, the way an add-on to a house has brick or aluminum siding that matches perfectly, seamlessly. The nest was easily mistaken for a knot in the tree. It was made of fibers and lint and dust sprinkled with chips of bark. Kio was pleased.

"I would have never seen that if you hadn't pointed it out. Look how well it's camouflaged!"

That's the day Kio offered to drive me home after work. We stopped for a drink at a lounge along the way. I ordered a glass of wine and she ordered a glass with ice. She swished it around like a frozen tornado, creating a climate of her own beneath the dry rim. She didn't suck on the ice. She didn't chew on it. She wasn't even waiting for the ice to melt so she could gulp down a shot's worth of cold water. Just kept the cubes spinning.

"I'll tell you my secrets if you tell me your dreams," I said. She put down her glass. "There's only one problem with a first love, Kio—you think it's going to be your last. I can't tell you how many nights I go to bed with a slice of cucumber over my eyes to help stop the swelling."

"So you know how to cry."

"I don't know how to stop."

Kio nodded, then began fingering the rim of her glass. Cubes melted down to featherweight chips. The napkin underneath was damp from sweat. When her hands began dripping with water, she told me everything I already knew: she was in love with her boss, she was a recovering alcoholic, he was too.

"You still haven't told me your dreams," I said as we got up to leave.

We walked out of the lounge to her car. She unlocked my door, grabbed the handle, and opened it before she spoke. "I wish for a day when I'll feel pure again."

We didn't say a word on the drive home until she pulled into

Dorothy's driveway. The sun hadn't set yet. "Want to come and see if I have any visitors?" I asked Kio.

"Sure."

"Wait here. I'll go check."

It was quiet at the feeder. I was disappointed but then I remembered the green feather I'd kept in the glass for good luck. I ran inside, put it in my hand, and closed it. I stood in front of the window and pictured Kio's dream. My fingers began to twitch. When I opened them, a hummer flew to the feeder.

I ran back to the car and signaled for Kio to park. When she walked into the apartment and spotted the bird, she took off her thick glasses. We saw every speck of color on every feather on its body. Its eyes shone like rivets. It flew backwards and forwards, nose diving before it darted past the feeder to a cupped leaf I placed on the windowsill that morning to catch the drizzle. We hurried to bring in two chairs from the kitchen and watched as the bird bathed its tiny body long after the rain had stopped.

Giovanna's 86 Circles

R eady, set, go." I held my breath while Marty counted. "One
thousand one. One thousand two . . ." I spewed the air
from my mouth and then counted for Marty. It turned
out neither of us were gonna be good kissers. Even fourth graders
like me knew the longer you could hold your breath, the better you
could kiss.

As we sat next to the old radiator against the wall of the vacant
Calderone farmhouse, we forgot about kissing when Marty pointed
out ring stains all over the hardwood floors. There were more on the
fireplace mantel and the windowsills.

"Wonder what these circles are from?"

"I was hoping you'd ask," he said, explaining that we were in the
sunroom where Giovanna Calderone kept all her potted plants. His
nonna knew Mrs. Calderone when she lived here and told him stories about her. He said he learned them off by heart because he was
thinking about reciting them here and charging admission since his
parents cut his allowance. He asked me to imagine that I was a paying audience. I said sure, so he ushered me to a seat, pretended to
hand me a program, and cleared his throat before he began.

"There once was a woman named Giovanna Calderone whose

plants grew faster than anybody else's around. She didn't have to water or weed or prune. She never planted seeds yet crops sprung up in her soil," he said, waving his hands above his head.

"All she had to do was put bushels under the peach trees so when the fruit was ripe, it rolled down the trunk into the basket without bruising. She'd shake the berry bushes until they all landed in her bowl as if it were a magnet. For every bunch of lilacs she picked, a dozen grew back. And the Swiss chard. You could stomp it into the ground, yet it bounced right back good as new. The roots on her rhubarb got so thick and long, they grew out of the drainpipe. That's because Giovanna braided them."

Marty waited to see if I was still paying attention.

"She had so much produce that she set up a little fruit stand close to the church on Sundays. When people came out of Mass, they bought up her peach jam and rhubarb pies, her berry tarts and pickled greens. Everyone wondered how she grew all this without a tractor or a hired hand or even a hoe. They asked Giovanna for her secret. All she ever told them was that she watered them."

"Yeah, but with what?"

Marty grinned. "I'll tell you when the others get here."

It was Marty's idea for our gang to have its clubhouse in the abandoned farmhouse. Before that, we hung out on the street by the mailbox and sewer. The boys thought it was cool to spit through the grate while the girls took turns climbing up the mailbox. The neighbors didn't want us there, though, because we made too much noise and played hide and seek in their bushes. So we built a treehouse in the woods, hanging a bullrope to swing off in case of an emergency. Then Marty showed us the inside of the Calderone farmhouse.

Not long after my best friend Sally joined me in the sunroom, Marty walked back in to hand her a small white box with a note folded in the shape of a triangle—the kind you play paper football with in homeroom. Sally opened the lid and found a boy's ring wrapped with lots of green angora yarn still on the band—probably left over from Tori, the girl Joey just broke up with. All the boys gave big rings to go steady, which meant girls had to pad the backs of the bands with soft yarn until they fit. Sally forced the ring past her knuckle.

"She's wearing it," Marty yelled to Joey, who was waiting in the next room. Sally opened the note. In shaky black letters floating between the lines, it read, "Dear Sally, I love you. Your friend, Joseph Drescher."

A few minutes later, Marty dragged Joey to the doorway, pushed him toward Sally, and signaled for them to go to another room. She spit out her fireball and handed it to me in a wrapper.

"You finish it," she said, tying the drawstrings on her wind-breaker real tight as she took Joey's hand.

"They're going to neck," Marty told me. "Do you think they make a good couple?"

"Yeah, they look like they wear the exact same shoe size."

Marty got up to put his ear on a hole in the flowered wallpaper. "I can hear them kissing," he said.

"But kissing doesn't make noise, Marty."

"If you're a beginner, it does."

I walked over to the hole in the wall and listened for myself. "I al-ready told you my big sister Rosemary says you have to be able to hold your breath for a whole minute if you want to be a good kisser. Like an underwater diver."

Since Marty talked in long sentences, he always took deep breaths, but I still wasn't sure what it'd be like to kiss him. He was skinny like me, so I knew at least I wouldn't have trouble wrapping my arms around him. His skin was dark like a freckle even when it wasn't summer. His eyelashes were as long as a spider's legs, and I had wondered if they would tickle in the middle of a kiss. And Marty's hair was real straight. It grew from the center of his head in different directions and reminded me of the spokes of a bicycle tire. What I'd thought I'd like best about kissing him was that he closed his eyes when he was afraid, not just for himself but for other people. Back in first grade, when Sister Mary Augusta lifted me up on my desk and made me do the twist to Chubby Checker in front of the class, I looked at him or down at my patent leather shoes.

"Wished we could see," Marty put his eye on the hole. "Dang, nothin'."

"Then finish your story about Giovanna if they're busy kissing. I'll tell you how much you should charge for it."

"I was hoping at least fifty cents. Think that's too much?"

"Get to the end and I'll tell you."

"Where was I? Oh, yeah. The year the drought killed all the crops, Giovanna sprinkled hers with the most powerful kind of water there is. Do you know what?"

I shook my head.

"Tears," he said, stretching the word as long as he could. "That year, her peaches were as big as grapefruits. Her berries were the size of apricots, and her chard and rhubarb were as tall as cornstalks. As she walked the field, she splashed tears on the crops like a priest does holy water up and down the church aisles. As a matter of fact, her fruit kept growing even after it was plucked from the trees. Didn't dry up no matter what. Stayed nice and juicy, so the only way you could stop it from getting any bigger was to eat it. And those are my nonna's exact words. I know 'cause I asked her to tell me the story enough times. The end."

"But where'd all the tears come from?"

"Praying, I guess."

"You mean 'cause she did something wrong and was hoping for forgiveness?"

"Not exactly."

I asked him why else you'd cry when you're saying "Hail Marys" and "Our Fathers."

"Maybe because she was happy."

"Nobody cries when they're happy," I told Marty. "Unless they have a really good reason. Like my dad. He cried when the Steelers won the Super Bowl and so does my aunt any time she wins the door prize at the Bingo."

"Nonna said Giovanna could cry walking through a field. Just like that!" He snapped his fingers and went on with the story, raising and lowering his voice for effect. "Oh, and I forgot. Her tears dropped in the buttercups the way water from a leaky roof drops in a bucket. One tear landed on every single leaf. Each trickled down a stem, and all the tears on the stems dropped to the trunk until a waterfall rushed down. It flooded the land with so much water that whatever wasn't attached to roots got washed away. My nonna says that's why Mr. Calderone rolled up his pantlegs before he left the house. Violets sprung up through the cement. Buttercups spread across the fields. Even the flowers on this here wallpaper came from Giovanna's tears."

"But look at this place now. It's one big weed, Marty."

"Don't say that."

"It's true!"

You couldn't see the peach grove or lilacs unless you climbed up the weeping willow. The berry bushes were all thorns and no fruit. The rhubarb and chard were buried under brush. We had to cut a path through to get to the farmhouse, which was rotting on the inside and out. The floorboards were practically sawdust. The green paint on the outside was all chipped off, and slabs of slate fell from the roof.

Even though nobody had lived in the house for years, Marty said his nonna thinks the Calderone spirits are still there. Fingerprints smudged the window seats. The edge of the stairs were smooth and round from all the footsteps. In the kitchen, a milk bottle with a red lid sat in the cupboard. There were melted wax candles in a closet. And all those water stains from the pots of plants keep getting darker in the sunroom.

"Let's count them," I said. I started at one end and Marty at the other and we worked our way to the middle. He was using his pointer finger to count. Before we knew it, he bumped my foot.

"How many?" I asked.

"Forty-four. And you?"

"Forty-three, counting this one."

"Then change mine to forty-three. I counted that one too."

"So there's eighty-six circles all together."

Marty smiled. "Now I get it."

"Get what?"

"One circle for each year," he explained.

"What do you mean, Marty?"

"Giovanna died when she was eighty-six."

"No lie?"

"That's what Nonna told me."

We were both hovering around Giovanna's eighty-sixth circle because neither of us wanted to leave it, and yet we were awful close to each other. Close enough to kiss. We had to do something—I chewed the rest of Sally's fireball as Marty took his pointer finger and traced it around and around the eighty-sixth circle.

"What do you think she planted in the pot that used to be there?" I asked.

Marty told me to guess, but I couldn't stop staring at his lips forming words. Then just his lips.

"I'm thinking," I was stalling for time. "Daffodils. That's what I'd plant. Or roses for a big boquet."

"My mom likes those," Marty said. "I know what I'd plant. A gardenia. Giovanna's would grow to the ceiling and the room would be a bottle of perfume. Ever smell one?"

"Sure I have. My sister wears Avon cream sachet. She even wears perfumed lipstick. Fruit flavors, though."

Marty and I stared down at the circle. He was probably picturing a gardenia on that spot and I was trying to see daffodils, but I still had Marty's lips on my mind. When we looked up, our heads bumped. I don't know how, but I remembered what my sister told me. She said kissing was easy. All you had to do was pretend you were licking a postage stamp. She didn't tell me the person you were kissing would pretend the same thing. Marty and I ended up with two tongues and no postage stamps. I wondered where our lips were supposed to be in all this.

The kiss was finished almost as soon as it started because I knew if you lick a postage stamp too long, it gets soggy. I was glad to get it over with. Maybe next time I'd like kissing as much as I liked being in Giovanna's sunroom. It was dipped in yellow, my favorite color, and the heat from the sun made me stretch out my arms, as if I had butterfly wings. I liked staring at all the empty circles, filling them in with my thoughts.

"Come on. Let's tell Sally and Joey," Marty said.

My mouth dropped. "About what?"

"The eighty-six circles. Let's have a séance."

Marty rounded up Sally and Joey to bring back Giovanna's spirit. We were all lying on the floor in a big circle, but first we traded hard rock candy. Everyone emptied out their quarter-pound bags, sliding pieces on the floor in someone's direction. I got the watermelon ones. Sally took the cinnamon, her favorite when she wasn't sucking on fireballs. Marty, the cherry. Joey, everything else. The clerk at G.C. Murphy's where we got it didn't allow us to pick through the mix for our favorite flavors so we each bought a quarter pound bag and traded.

Marty lit a votive candle and set it on the floor in the middle of the eighty-sixth water stain. We formed a perfect circle. I took Sally's hand and felt the furry lump of angora from her ring.

"Your hands are cold," she complained.

Before I held Marty's hand, I ran mine across my pants to wipe off the sweat and tried warming it up between my legs. Turns out it didn't matter though because Marty's hand was as cold and clammy as mine.

Sally was still giggling about Joey. "We kissed," she whispered.

I didn't want to say anything about mine. I knew she'd just ask me questions that I didn't have answers for, so I kept thinking about the eighty-six circles in the sunroom and how Giovanna got her plants to grow.

Everyone grew quiet. The candle began to flicker, and I could feel a draft coming from the doorway. The glass doorknob against the dark wood looked like a full moon in a midnight sky. I thought I saw it turn when Marty spoke up.

"Close your eyes everybody and listen. I hear Giovanna. She's coming over to us. She wants to say something."

Joey turned to Marty. "Lay it on me."

"Keep holding hands. She likes our circle."

"All right!" Loud and clear, man," Joey said.

"Everyone get up," Marty instructed.

"I thought you said she liked it?"

"She does, but we have to make more circles. Around the house." Marty told us we had to take turns running circles around the house. Eighty-six times.

"That's too many," Joey complained. "Can't we just neck instead?"

Sally slapped Joey's arm.

"I got another idea. Let's dance to 'Hey, Jude' instead," he said.

"Let's run," Marty shouted as he led us around the house.

We finished four laps before Marty stopped to pick up a sign that blew over. It said new houses were going to be built on the property.

"You lie!" said Joey.

"Could it be a mistake?" I asked.

Marty led us back to the sunroom for a séance to ask Giovanna's spirit about the sign. We held hands and waited. Finally, he said, "I see her. She's sitting on the window seat looking outside at the peach grove and the lilacs."

Marty was quiet for a few seconds. "Now she's crying."

"Why?" I asked.

"Now she's getting up to sniff her flowers!"

I told Marty to ask her if they're going to tear it down.

"I can't get her attention."

"I know. Let's set booby traps," Sally said.

"Ah, man. That won't work," Joey said.

Marty made us all run home and bring back shovels. Twenty minutes later, we started digging a ditch around the property so the bulldozers wouldn't be able to get through. When Sally and Joey weren't listening, I asked Marty if Giovanna was crying hard. He told me she was but not because she was sad. I wasn't sure if I believed him.

After a few scoops of soil, we began to hit roots that were so knotted together it was impossible to pick up any dirt.

"Ah, man. Can this wait?" Joey asked.

"It's getting dark. We can't see what we're doing," Sally said.

We gave up and went home with a plan to come back the next day. That night, I dreamed that Marty and I had our shovels and were digging up all of Giovanna's trees and bushes to replant them someplace where they'd be safe. We kept digging and digging and just like what really happened, we hit a wall of roots. I reached down to try and pull them out and heard a scream. I remember looking into a deep ditch and seeing Giovanna way down there sitting in a chair with a bunch of curly roots on her lap. She had a giant rake to comb out all the tangles and knots until the roots were perfectly straight. She separated them into three piles, took one bunch on the right and put it over the bunch in the middle. Then she took the bunch on the left and put that over the middle, braiding them the way you do hair. I waited for Giovanna to reach the end. She never did because she kept crying on the roots and they kept growing.

Climbing down the hole to stand right beside her, I looked into her eyes to see if Marty was right—if she was crying because she was happy. I still couldn't tell. I put my hand on her cheek, but her tears never touched me. I even tried moving my hand to catch one but couldn't. What was worse, I was crying and couldn't feel my own tears.

The next day, Marty and I stopped by the Calderone house after school and saw a man surveying the land and pounding in posts at the edge of the property. He said everything would be razed. We asked if they could build around Giovanna's house, but he shook his head and laughed.

"There's a neat sunroom in there, you know," Marty told the man.

"I don't think the new houses will have those."

We kept hounding him until he let us know when they were scheduled to tear it down. Marty asked me if I wanted to cut school that day. I told him I had a math test, but the truth was I didn't want to watch. I even walked to school a different way so I didn't have to pass by. Marty kept telling me I had to see it, but I made excuses until one day he grabbed me by the hand and took me there.

Giovanna's farmhouse was leveled. The soil was bare. I could see every hump and every crack in the ground like a shaved scalp. The land already formed a layer of crust. Soon after, cement foundations covered the soil and shells for the new houses were built.

To get inside, you had to walk a plank over an eight-foot ditch into a house covered with plywood on the floor and two by fours where walls would be. Pink insulation was stuffed between beams and looked like flesh next to bone. It was nothing like Giovanna's sunroom. I wanted to leave as soon as I got there, but Sally and Joey didn't seem to notice as much because they were busy necking.

Marty and I ended up together again. He led me by the hand to a certain room. I didn't know why. They all looked the same to me. I told him I wanted to leave.

"Do you know where we are?"

I shrugged my shoulders. "Where?"

"Giovanna's sunroom."

I looked around but didn't see anything familiar. "No, we're not."

He pointed at the window. "I walked home from school and saw the sun shine through at the same angle as it did her sunroom. It has to be."

"It's dark in here, Marty. Nothing like her sunroom."

He pulled out a piece of wood and handed it to me. It took me a second to figure out that it was one of the eighty-six circles from Giovanna's sunroom.

He spoke softly. "I got this for you. I think it's the middle one, but I'm not sure."

I took it and started to cry, wiping the tears on my sleeve.

"I'm sorry. I didn't think it would make you sad," he said.

I didn't know if I was crying because there was no sunroom or farm that Giovanna grew with her tears, or because I was glad that someone felt the same as me. I didn't know that Marty cared enough to sneak back in and get the exact circle we both counted, the circle where we kissed, the circle where Giovanna made everything grow.

"Marty, I think I'm crying because I'm happy," I said.

"I was hoping you'd say that!"

I reached over and planted a kiss dead center on his lips. It felt so much better than the first one. Maybe because I wasn't thinking about postage stamps.

I thought I heard the rumble of an earthquake. The cement floor seemed to split in two and a huge gardenia bush popped up. When it reached the ceiling, it poked a hole in it and kept growing until it came out through the roof. All around us, concrete crumbled, and Giovanna's plants grew back. The peach groves appeared with fuzzy orange fruit. The lilacs had more purple flowers on them than leaves. The field was golden again with buttercups. The stems of the rhubarb were as red as ever. The bushes dropped all their thorns and berries grew in their place.

I could see construction workers swearing to the police that they tore the roots clean out. Rumors would spread that Giovanna's spirit was taking back her land. Homeowners would say the place was haunted and threaten to get their money back. Marty would lead tours and charge two dollars a head. Everybody would want to know just how this could happen, but there wasn't any way to explain it. The answer was smack in middle of Giovanna's eighty-sixth circle and Marty's lips.

The Drying Corner

I never thought of my grandmother as old, but for the first time she acted old. Moving slow, head to the ground, drooping like a puppet. The cane she used for her bad knee was ready to snap from all her weight. I helped her up the stairs to her front porch, through the kitchen door and into the living room where she sat down on that easy chair she liked so much. As a girl everyone called "skinny minny," I wasn't supposed to be able to do that. I guess I still had that juice in me from my drying corner. It filled me with so much energy, I didn't know what to do with it all. And it emptied out Nonna so she had none.

I didn't mean for it to turn out that way. It's just that everybody was talking about the fruit store closing, and I knew how much that would upset Nonna. I was trying real hard to make her see that when it happened, I'd make it so there was a little something left behind. It seems as though everybody in Tarentum is either leaving or dying—whichever comes first. Two of my friends had to move away when their daddy's movie house closed down. The best part about going with them to the Manos was getting the twenty-five-cent buttered popcorn for free. We'd cover the tub with a napkin and shake it so all the kernels got some, even the ones at the bottom. Now the

Manos is a liquor store, which is mean because I'm not too old for popcorn, but I'm way too young to drink. That leaves kids like me with nothing.

Nonna always said I was even too young to be drying up herbs and flowers and fruit peels. She said a girl my age should dream about the same things other eleven year olds did in all the river towns up the Allegheny—like shave my legs, learn how to drive, bake snicker doodles, and wear a padded bra. She never asked me, but I had my thoughts all ready for her just in case she did. Shaving your legs only brought nubs, and I'd rather have soft hairs poking out my fishnets than stiff ones. And what good was a driver's license without a car? My dad said if I wanted wheels when I turned sixteen, he'd put a horn on my bicycle. Baking snicker dickers—that's what I called them—was not my idea of fun because I always forgot to put the sugar in. Nobody ate them, so I had to because Mom said I couldn't keep wasting ingredients. Padded bras? That'd be like stuffing cotton candy down my shirt. I told Nonna I'm not going to wear those no matter how little I was.

"Even if you're the size of a plum?" she asked.

I shook my head.

"An apricot?"

"No!"

"What about those little cherries I sell at the store, Lorna?"

"I'm already bigger than that. Besides, they're nice and juicy."

Nonna cracked a smile and squeezed my arm like she was feeling a piece of fruit to see how ripe it was, then she pinched it. Her hands were rough, her knuckles big, and her grip strong.

"You ain't kiddin', honey. Got to have juice."

"What are you gonna do if the store closes? Mom heard the new mall off the freeway is bigger than all of downstreet. She says you might as well die when that happens."

"I ain't goin' nowhere. I'm staying put," she said as she sprung up to greet Adam, the deliveryman. I believed my mother more than I did Nonna and decided I better start making a drying corner

66

before the fruit store closed down for good. I figured it would look the same as Miller's Business Supplies, a vacant store right across the street with dusty adding machines in the window.

Bad business downstreet was spreading like a rash of poison ivy. First Kumer's bakery closed down. Cogley's jewelers went next. Everybody said that was just an accident that two stores in a row went out of business. Then Schenken's furniture store on the other side of Cogley's and Weisburg's butcher shop beside Schenken's closed their doors. Now my mom says everyone's waiting for Berky's dress shop to go next because it's beside the butcher. Then it'll be our place, DiGirolamo's fruit store, my mom said.

I asked my mom how come this is happening and she said it all started with Kumer's coconut cream pie. When the bakery closed down, why go to Cogley's to get your watch fixed if you couldn't buy that luscious mound of meringue with coconut sprinkled on top? Why buy a lampshade at Schenken's when you can't get your watch fixed or the pie? And no sense in picking up your city chickens at Weisburg's—even though they're on the stick ready to bread and fry—if you can't get the shade, the watch, or the pie.

Nonna says this kind of talk is superstitious, and she doesn't believe it, but then why does she wear her clothes inside out and backwards when she goes to the Bingo? You can't see the seams and the tags on her jersey because she's got a smock buttoned on top, so she does it just the same when she works.

The mirrors in my grandma's fruit store made it look twice as big, and footsteps tapdanced on the hardwood floors, sounding as if there were more people than ever. The floors smelled good—like a Popsicle stick after I licked it clean. What I liked best about the place was how many things I could turn upside down and dry for Nonna when she wasn't looking. I was saving it all for her, but she didn't know that.

Every Saturday when I came to help, I kept an eye on the fresh bunches of herbs and flowers on a stand I set up outside. I hounded Nonna to let me have them if they didn't sell that day. I told her that no way half-dead herbs and flowers would make it through the weekend and I wasn't going to let them wilt for nobody except the garbage collector.

"What on earth are you going to do with those?" Nonna asked.

"I'm gonna keep them."

"Whatever for, Lorna?"

"So I don't have to throw them out. You'll see."

"What's a girl your age going to do with those?"

I tried sneaking off with an artichoke. Figured it would probably go bad before she sold it.

"Put that back," she snapped. "I can get a good price for those."

She used to anyway. For just about everything and that was a lot. The fruit store was a jungle. She had produce hanging from the ceiling—bananas, garlic, hot peppers, all kinds of ribbons and wicker baskets she filled with fruit so customers could give them as gifts to sick people. Mom said Nonna still overstocked the place because she expected the same number of customers as she had twenty years ago, but how could she when her customers were the ones in the hospital now?

I pretended the ribbons were snakes and dodged them, so I didn't get poisoned to death. She had every kind of basket dangling from an old broomstick near the ceiling—some so low that when tall people like Uncle Ray walked through, they brushed against his head. Being that he was a barber across the street, he always pulled out a comb from his back pocket and tucked the loose hairs under a blanket of grease. And on hot days when the fan was on high, the baskets blew around so much that he said the store needed a traffic cop. I just bet there was a time when there were more paying customers than baskets. Maybe when the Manos had a live organist on Saturday nights and buttered popcorn.

"Lorna's here today, Ray."

I wish she wasn't a blabbermouth with him around. I dropped what I was doing and snuck to the back room or else he'd ask me for a kiss. Personally, I thought Nonna made him nag me all the time just to get my mind off drying herbs and flowers.

I was lucky. He wanted to talk over business with her, but that scared me almost as much as kissing him. He talked about the mall and sounded just like Mom did about it.

"All that's going to be left to Tarentum are doctor's offices and funeral parlors. You wait and see."

"Ah, bullshit," Nonna said.

"How many sales today, Nellie?"

"Who's counting?"

Uncle Ray knew he wasn't going to get anywhere with Nonna. "Where's Peewee hiding? Don't I get a kiss today?"

I shoulda just given him one to get it over with because thinking about it the whole time was a lot worse. At least I could count on a barber having smooth skin and aftershave lotion. But the best thing about giving Uncle Ray a kiss was that I could get back to finding something to dry. I gave him one. Didn't move my lips though.

Since Nonna had Uncle Ray on her side to keep me from my drying corner, I decided I needed Aunt Philly on mine to help me escape to it. Most times, she was no match for Nonna, like when they marked a price on the bag, she always finished first because she put her red pen on her ear and Aunt Philly kept hers in a big pocket. She had to fish in there and would pull out a tissue or candy wrapper first. Aunt Philly may have been slower than Nonna, but at least she had a soft spot. Nonna was as hard as an avocado seed when it came to business.

I built my drying corner outside the back of the store, using four big nails I spotted beside the cash register that Aunt Philly pocketed for me. Once I hammered them in a wall, I tied a piece of ribbon on each one. Then all I needed was something to dry. I went back inside and found Nonna pulling out a bunch of splinters she got dragging a cantaloupe crate. Aunt Philly always hollered at her for not wearing gloves.

"Nonna, I have something to show you, but first I want you to promise me you won't say *fatti un monaco'* or whatever it is you say in Italian to tell me to get lost."

"Make it quick."

I took her to the herb and flower buckets and told her a lie so I could get her to give me something. "A customer just walked by and said how old everything looked."

"Where?"

"She was going to buy parsley and didn't."

Nonna pulled a homely bunch out of a bucket of water and plucked off a few yellow leaves. Even she couldn't make it look good. She handed it to me and said, "That's it."

The parsley looked a little lost when I hung it to dry in my corner, but all I could think about was this itching that started inside me like ants crawling around in there. It made it hard for me to stay put.

Nonna brought out a red magic marker and some cardboard. She just raised the price of cherries. "Make me some new signs while you're waiting for that parsley to dry."

I told Nonna I could just make the seven into an eight on the old ones, but she said she didn't want her customers to see she upped the price ten cents—bad for business. And business was bad enough. Aunt Philly was just the opposite. She always threw in more than the order called for because she said people were hurting. They couldn't afford to shop at a specialty store for produce anymore.

"Phil," Nonna called out.

"Yeah, Nick." That was my grandma's nickname for Nellie, which was a nickname for Carmella, but nobody called her that.

"Mrs. Betish's order has to be ready by noon. She's picking it up on the way to the beauty shop."

"Right-o," Aunt Philly said, rubbing on hand lotion. She always squirted on too much and tried to give the extra to Nonna who sure could have used it. Never worked because Nonna didn't let nothin' get in the way of her grip. She said the produce slid right out of her hand.

She noticed how Aunt Philly picked up the first tomato, then put it down and picked up another one. She knew the hand lotion wasn't to blame either. Aunt Philly looked up and saw Nonna's eyes staring at her.

"You know how Mrs. Betish is."

"You spoil her, so you do," Nonna muttered.

Aunt Philly turned to me. "What are you going to do? She's one of the few customers we have who doesn't buy on credit."

I hung a few bruised cherries that I found in a bushel and some snapdragons too and felt this tingling in my body again as I tied them on nails. I ran back in.

"You should see what I put in Dr. Lifkin's bag—the same thing as I put in everyone else's," Nonna insisted.

Aunt Philly turned to me and said, "He used to chase her along the river when she was young. The only way she got rid of him was by jumping in."

"That jasper couldn't swim and I could." Nonna explained as she grabbed a crowbar and yanked open a crate of corn for me to husk. I could see her swimming muscle in the back of her arm, but then it disappeared.

I had a hard time keeping still. It was like I ate too much candy. I wanted to jump up and touch the baskets and swing on bunches of bananas. Do cartwheels too. Nonna noticed because she had me running to the back of the store carrying orders to Adam, who was loading up the delivery truck. She never had me do that before because the bags were heavy.

She said she was too busy, but I saw she looked tired even though every night she still downed her hot milk spiked with rum to get a good night's rest. It put her to sleep and so did listening to radio voices, especially sports. They made her snore.

I knew she was tuckered, but I asked Nonna to take me to the bathroom down in the basement because it was dark and she knew where to switch on the light. She didn't mind. It gave her the chance to try and keep me from staring at the pictures of naked women the men from the warehouse hung up by the stairs.

"Look. They're the size of grapefruit, huh?"

"Never you mind, Lorna. Watch where you're going." Nonna held onto the railing and me as we climbed down. I swore if it weren't for those pictures of naked women, she wanted to rest between steps real bad.

The next Saturday was even worse. When I hung up a red pepper Aunt Philly saved for me, Nonna fell asleep eating lunch. She always ate standing up so she could get back to work even faster than having to lift herself off a stool—that's what we called a crate turned on its side and padded on top with wrapping paper and big gum bands around it.

I couldn't believe she kept an eggplant sandwich waiting like that. It was her favorite. Better than steak, she said. I tapped her on the shoulder. "Aren't you going to finish?"

"I don't know what's the matter with me today," she answered. "I need a good strong cup of coffee, so I do."

She usually poured herself one and dunked a cookie in her tazza, but I offered to get it for her.

"I'll make it nice and strong."

I snuck a flask of whiskey one of the customers kept in a cabinet, poured some in her cup, and brought it over to her.

She took a sip and stopped. "What'd you put in here?"

"I said I made it strong for you. Drink up now."

She put the cup down. "Needs more sugar. Come on. Let's go."

"Will you make me an eggnog when we get home?"

"I thought you didn't like 'em?"

"I'll drink one if you do."

"Bullshit. You won't even watch me crack the egg."

"You want skinny minny to gain weight, don't ya?"

"Get goin'!"

We passed a big willow tree to get to her house and walked along the railroad tracks on Sixth Avenue where all the big stores in Tarentum were. My grandma said you used to have to wait to cross there were so many trains back and forth to Pittsburgh.

"Everybody took a train. To Jenkins Arcade. To the Strip District. To Kaufman's. To Moio's Bakery in East Liberty for cannoli."

"Now we have to wait a long time to see a train, don't we, Nonna?"

She didn't answer. She complained of a headache and made me get her some pills at the drug store. I knew she must have felt bad because she held onto her cane real tight instead of using it to swat me on my rear end. The willow tree we always passed had roots growing under the sidewalk—so many of them that the slate slabs made a hill we had to climb. While I was doing cartwheels, Nonna's cane got stuck in the crack at the top. She lost her balance and fell on her bad knee.

"Are you okay, Nonna?"

"I'm going to have them chop that damn tree down. If it's the last thing I do. God willing, I'll live another day to do it."

She never talked like that. I couldn't figure out what was happening to her. All I knew was it started after I built my drying corner. I did something I don't usually do with Nonna. I didn't ask first. I picked her up and helped her walk the rest of the way home. While she rested on her easy chair with her feet propped up on her hassock, she told me to switch on all the lights even though it wasn't dark, turn on the kitchen radio even though she wasn't going to pay it any mind, and do all kinds of things to make the place seem lived in. She had me boil a pot of coffee, pull out the chairs from the table, take her Bingo chips out and put a few on an old card, hang a Sunday dress outside the closet, put her garden gloves on the table. If it were my room, my mama would have taken one look and yelled at me for being too lazy to pick up after myself. Nonna sat in the chair and didn't move. Not a word either. I didn't know what to think except that her whole house was turned on, but she was turned off.

I got the idea then and there. I wanted to chop the willow tree down myself. This way she wouldn't have to walk up and down the sidewalk no more and trip like she did. I always liked that willow, the way its shoelace branches dangled back and forth like someone trying to hypnotize me. I liked hugging its limbs when I climbed it.

They were the color of bearskin and had big grooves like thick corduroy. If I looked real close, I saw ants crawling, a whole other world down there while I had mine. And we didn't get in each other's way. I liked the willow, but I didn't like how it made Nonna feel. She wasn't herself.

Later, I dreamed I ran to my drying corner and touched everything I had hanging. I had enough juice in me to cut down the willow with one good chop. I held my ears tight when it hit the brick street. I dragged it to my corner, roots and all, and turned it upside down to dry. Nonna was watching me. A parsley flake from my bunch blew over to her and landed on her thumb, snapping it off and carrying it above the fruit store awning and then higher until I couldn't see it anymore. The cherries I had drying shriveled up to pits and floated over to her eyes. Her arms and legs got flat and curled under. The trunk on the willow knotted up as if it were a shirt somebody was wringing out, and the water dripping from it became a giant pool. I turned and saw that the paper from the adding machines on display in the abandoned storefront wrapped itself around Nonna like a mummy. I reached over to touch her when suddenly the paper around her came unraveled and fell to the ground like a slip you drop over your hips. There was nothing left of her when she jumped into the pool feet first. I waited for her to surface. She did, but she was a young woman now. She lifted her arms in the shape of an arrow and dove straight down this time. Her feet were the last thing I saw. I heard bubbles at the other end of the pool and then nothing. I wanted to touch her, but I was afraid if I did, she'd shrivel up again.

When I got up the next morning, I knew what I had to do. For Nonna. I left my house early and hurried to the drying corner to take everything down. I stuffed the dried herbs and flowers in my knee socks and book bag and ran to her house. She was making breakfast. I was relieved to see her usual two pieces of Italian toast and half a grapefruit on the table. She had on the apron she wore at the store.

"Are you better, Nonna?"

She made the sign of the cross as she said, "Thank God. I'm ready for work." I believed her more when she fixed her half grape-fruit like she always does. She only cut every other section so you had to fiddle with your spoon to get it out. Mom cut every section so it slipped right out. That was just like Nonna to make herself work for everything, even a piece of grapefruit.

The dried herbs and flowers got so itchy in my knee socks that I scratched all the way to the fruit store after school. Uncle Ray was there. "What have you got there, Peewee?"

"You better watch out for that granddaughter of mine, Ray. She'll hang you upside down by the toes and put you out to dry if you're not careful," Nonna said. He must have taken her seriously because he didn't stoop down for a kiss.

I went to the backroom and glued all the dried things onto the back of an old sign—the one for cherries before Nonna raised the price. I showed her what I'd made when she was eating lunch.

"So this is what you do."

"Can you tell? It's a picture of you."

Nonna stepped back and put her hands on her cheeks. "Will you look at that? Pomegranate skins for my cheeks."

"It's the color of your rouge."

"And snapdragons for my hair?"

"Since you got your permanent." I knew that wasn't the answer she wanted. "I took 'em when you weren't looking."

Her face popped out from behind the piece of cardboard. "You little turd."

She noticed the corn silk and the beet stems I used to make her red-striped smock.

"You can keep it, Nonna," I said as she hung it above the table where she made her fruit baskets. "It's going to last. Longer than the fruit store will."

Uncle Ray walked into the backroom to tell Nonna a customer said Berky's dress shop was closing next door. He was wondering about his barbershop. All the while, Nonna didn't say a word. I was hoping she'd look at my picture.

I kept my eye on her and decided it meant more to her than she let on. After Uncle Ray left, she stared at it and gently ran her fingers over the different textures and shapes like she wanted to learn another way to touch besides squeezing a piece of fruit to see how ripe it was. She looked out to the storefront and didn't see any customers.

She signaled me to come help. "Lorna, we've got to get the honeydews into the cooler. They've been sitting out too long."

She didn't waste time handing me a bruised one. I was ready to toss it out, and for a minute I wondered if she gave it to me to dry. I thought of asking her if I could, but it turned out I was glad I didn't. She cut off the brown spots with her paring knife and sliced the melon up.

"Half each," she said, handing me two pieces. "We've got the best part right here. And you thought it was done for."

Nonna was right. That honeydew was so juicy and sweet, our hands were dripping.

Raw Egg in Beer

On the day he was to die, the mayor wore a crisp white shirt. It was bright enough to celebrate the absence of color and starched to ward off temptation from wrinkles. The brim of his Stetson looked like wings, and the diamond on his pinky shone as if it were crowned in a halo. He walked in to Major's Tavern at exactly 6:30 P.M., the same time he did every other day of the year. He sat on the same black vinyl barstool between the cash register and the wall in a coat-rack pose regulars could imitate. He ordered the same bottle of beer. This day would be no different, even if he had said it was his last. I reached in my purse for my reporter's notebook to jot all this down.

Although the mayor is eighty-six years old, he is in excellent health, according to his family doctor who tells me he could keep going for another fifteen years. He still has rosy cheeks, a gripping handshake, and endurance from swimming every morning. Then he goes to the nursing home and feeds, bathes, and dresses his wife, Elisabetta, who has been suffering from Alzheimer's for a number of years. Then it's off to work mornings at the borough office and afternoons at the bank he founded. He also owns a construction company and, time permitting, he visits development sites. Then he has a few drinks at the tavern before going home to change into a suit and tie if there's a council meeting that evening. And as a devoted Catholic, he confesses his sins and receives Holy Communion every Sunday and holy day.

Salvatore Taviani was so strong in his faith that he called our city editor, Renae Harper, and said he knew when he was going to die. He claimed he was privy to his time on earth much the same way the borough finance director apprised him of the balance in each and every line item of the borough's $2.6 million budget. I knew that doctors could predict death within weeks or even days for terminal patients but doubted how the mayor could predict the day of his death when he was in perfect health.

As the only Catholic on the reporting staff, I was assigned to cover the mayor's last day for the *Valley Daily Gazette*. Renae wouldn't listen when I said that I was a lapsed Catholic who hadn't been to Mass in so long that I wouldn't know when to sit or stand or kneel anymore. I told her it was one thing to print obits celebrating life but to ask me to write an article about somebody's death when they're still alive? And what insight could I possibly offer in my fallen state of grace?

She winked at me and said, "Keep the faith, Daria."

"It's a hoax," I snapped. "After all the calls I made, nobody could say for sure how the mayor knows except that as a life-long practicing Catholic, he's been given the word from 'above.' How's a reporter supposed to verify the facts when there are none? Only hunches."

And to make matters worse, the only reason I'm allowed to see the mayor at all is because Renae assured him that I wouldn't ask him about this. She had this idea that I'd buy him a few beers, get his tongue loose, and then fire all kinds of questions at him, which he'd start to answer before I even finished my sentence. Questions like what did he think was going to happen to him once he died? Is there life after death? Did knowing make a difference?

"Don't worry, Daria. You'll get him to talk. Catholic to Catholic," she said.

"What do I say? That I remember my first grade teacher Sister Mary Augusta telling us after Father Sullivan interrupted art class to announce President Kennedy's assassination that our time of death was only for the good Lord in his infinite wisdom to know? That we all folded our hands and bowed our heads in prayer to say the rosary, but I lost my place because I was too busy peeling the dried-up chips of paste off my fingertips? And that my faith has gone downhill ever since? Is that what I'm supposed to tell him—Catholic to Catholic?"

Renae said she'd bump ads, hold stories, and even take the masthead off the front page if need be to give me enough space to write the full story.

"What if it's not true?"

She raised her eyebrows.

I was a reporter, not a Catholic. I wanted a document, a study, a piece of paper that verified the alleged claim. A stone tablet would be nice—with or without the burning bush. I reminded Renae that our investigative team of reporters hadn't uncovered a trace of secondary evidence inferring an impending suicide. No closed bank accounts, funeral arrangements, wills, executive orders, or deed transfers. It made sense that as a staunch supporter of the Democratic machine, Taviani would have at least filled out an absentee ballot so as not to miss the upcoming election given that it was guaranteed to be a close race. They turned up nothing.

After she had me write half a dozen obituaries of people who we knew for a fact were dead, Renae shooshed me out the door to catch up with the mayor at Major's Tavern.

A pair of eyes peers through the blinds as I squeeze my car between a navy blue Olds and a dirt-brown Cutlass in the tavern parking lot. I'm a few minutes early so I plop myself down on a bar stool, one of the few empty seats in the house. The bartender doesn't say a word as he walks away from the window, but he looks at me as if I've done something wrong.

"Don't give her the evil eye now. How's she supposed to know?" says a woman as she tugs at the bartender's apron. She turns to me and explains, "If you sit there, you'll have to buy everybody drinks. That's where the mayor sits."

I leap up from my seat and slide over to face a jar of beef jerkies on the counter. "Sorry about that."

"Be nice to your customers, Greg," she says, pinching the bartender's cheek. "This here's Gregory and I'm Mimi."

I look back, and Mimi points to the oval hole in the linoleum bar rung where the mayor rests his right foot.

"Yeah, once Sal gets through the wood, we're going to close the place down," says Gregory. I wait for him to add that he has one more day to do it but he doesn't.

Gregory's wife Rita emerges from the back room with her hair in curlers long enough to say, "I'll take a saw to it and do it for him then." She is pulling out pink sponge from her hair.

White blinking Christmas lights trim the bar, which is black stained wood. Gregory says Rita had it varnished that way so fingerprints and dirt wouldn't show. He allowed her to do that if she let him keep the Christmas lights up year-round. When they flash on, Gregory's every move somehow seems worth watching. He dips a dirty glass in soapy water, then in a pan of running water before drying the inside with a tea towel and his hands with his apron. Suddenly, he's in the dark and I can only imagine what he's doing. Low ceiling fans with white paddles whir above our heads. The floor is a huge checkerboard. Gregory pulls out a mop and glides over the black squares, bearing down when he gets to the white ones. Rita has her hair sprayed stiff and is watering the Easter lily on the windowsill. She notices the trumpet flower is drooping, so she sets the sprinkling can on the table and tries to get the flower to face up. It goes limp as soon as she lets go.

I pull out my reporter's notebook from my pocket and explain that I'm writing a story on the mayor. I keep it casual.

"I love him. The mayor's blue eyes twinkle. They do," says Mimi, nursing a half-empty glass of red wine.

"That's a sign of good health," I say.

"Oh, he's a picture of health," Mimi smiles.

"I hear the doctor says he could live another twenty years. You agree?"

"Just about anything's possible."

Gregory cuts in by recalling the mayor's first job as a paperboy. Instead of walking the route or biking up hills, he bought a motorcycle with a sidecar attached where his brother sat tossing stacks of papers as he drove.

"Sal's parents were immigrants from Calabria," he continues. "The boot of Italy he calls it. He quit school in the eighth grade, you know, and worked in the coal mines with his father to help support the family. 'Course, he's practically a millionaire now, but he didn't start out that way."

Gregory tells me that after working in the coal mines, the mayor saved enough money to open up an auto repair shop and beer distributorship before his construction business. He began with a hammer, shovel, and cement trail and worked his way from cementing steps to building roads and bridges.

"What's he going to do with all his money?" I ask.

"Sal gives a lot of it away. I know that for a fact. He knows every single one of this borough's 26,000 people by their first name. Believe it, it's true."

Mimi laughs and adds, "Except for my daughter, Annamay. When she had her twelfth birthday, the mayor had the baker put Annamaria on the cake."

"Doesn't he know what her real name is?"

Mimi shakes her head and smiles. "Yeah, but he likes Annamaria better. I guess because he's Italian. Now everyone calls her that. I thought of changing her name. It would be a helluva lot easier, I tell ya."

A man at the bar taps me on the shoulder and whispers: "He's shrewd, all right. He soaks his friends and fellow businessmen in drink before bidding on a project. That's what he does. He rents a suite and throws a big party. I've been to one of them. Everyone except him drinks. He listens to them all talking numbers. And no sooner than when the last person leaves the room, he sits down at his desk and revises his own bid."

I approach Rich, a man in a suit and raincoat who tells me that he thought the mayor hated him when he was on the borough council. "We saw eye to eye on nothing, to the point where I thought of resigning," he admits.

"What changed that?"

"One hundred fifty dollars. The mayor and I came within one hundred fifty dollars of each other on the budget. Can you believe that? We think alike. Except he did his in his head in twenty minutes and it took me thirty-five hours to come up with mine."

"Maybe yunz don't think alike after all," Gregory says as he stacks clean glasses on the shelf.

"Well, I like him. Period," blurts out a man in a baseball cap and hunting vest and adds, before I get a chance to ask him, "The name's Al."

"What do you think about today?"

Al looks down and starts zipping and unzipping his vest.

"What about it?" says Gregory as a glass slips out of his hands and falls. He gets a broom and quickly sweeps up the pieces.

I keep waiting for someone to so much as acknowledge that they believe the mayor is going to die today like he says he is. I can't help but think that either they don't believe him or they're so faithful to him that they believe everything he says carte blanche—including the part about this day being no different.

I glance at my watch. It's 6:30 P.M. Sure enough, the mayor's standing at the doorway. He waits there for a few seconds before walking in. His full head of hair is slicked back as usual to flaunt a natural hairline that hadn't receded "as much as a gnat's eyelash" as Pittsburgh Pirate sportscaster Bob Prince used to say when an outfielder just missed catching a home run ball over the fence at Forbes Field.

"Hi, pal," Al greets him.

"Hey, Mr. Mayor," Rich calls out.

"We've been waiting for you," Mimi says.

The mayor smiles, "Same time, same station every day."

He sits on the black bar stool, leans against the wall, and positions his shiny black leather shoe on the bar rung right on top of the hole. His other foot dangles. His back is straight as he holds out a glass of beer in one hand while his other forms a loose fist suspended in air, the fingers wiggling as though he's playing a musical instrument. Within minutes, everyone huddles around him. I wait to see if they'll confront his death, once and for all. Even if it's just nagging questions such as who will take his place since he is the one and only mayor in the borough's fifty-year history.

Instead they talk about food. The menu changes from meatball sandwiches to veal cutlet.

"I'm taking orders," the mayor announces.

"What about veal? How many pounds, Sal?" Gregory asks.

The mayor's voice squeaks through the noise. "Let me mess with that."

Gregory chuckles. "That settles it. No skimping—veal parmesan, a side plate of pasta, salad, garlic bread, and two vegetables."

I'm convinced they're talking about his wake, but then I hear the mayor say, "The only ground rule is that you stay out of the kitchen while I cook."

Gregory says they're planning a hunting trip at his camp. I ask when. Everyone defers to the mayor. "When it always is. The first day of hunting."

"Don't forget to bring your horn now, Mr. Mayor," Al says.

"You don't want me to do that."

Gregory tells me that years ago, Taviani went to Canada on a moose hunting expedition with an Indian guide. At night, he got in a boat and blew a horn, waiting for the moose to come to the water's edge. He stood up to shoot, and the boat tipped over. The mayor was fished out of the frigid waters and had to stay beside a fire all night to keep from shivering to death.

"We're going to catch one this time," the mayor says. "Aren't we, Al?"

Al gives his dutiful reply. "If you say so, then we are, Mr. Mayor."

Gregory fills me in on a little camp history. "Sal has had camp parties for more than fifty years, back in the days when we had to work on our cars for a week to get them to run a two-hundred-mile trip. I've known him since I was a kid and every party he's ever had was good."

Rich gets up and walks over to the video screen after buying a roll of quarters from Gregory.

"Hey, since when isn't a video game a spectator sport?" shouts a woman at the bar stool who had just downed her third can of Pepsi.

"Oh, I'm sorry," Rich apologizes, moving his body to the other side of the screen so as not to block her view.

Once she thanks him, she turns to me and says, "You know this isn't right. I'm wearing a trench coat, and I'm fully clothed underneath."

I prod Rich. "Be honest with me. Are you all going to be here with the mayor tomorrow or not?"

"We do it every day," he shrugs.

"If this is his last day, how come nobody's acting like it? Do you believe him or don't you?"

A man sitting across from me suddenly taps me on the shoulder and says with a hostile tone, "Are you a Democrat or a Republican?"

"Does it matter?"

"It does to the mayor."

"Then tell me you haven't been looking ahead to the next election when the mayor's gone and the Republicans will have a shot this time to fill his seat."

"He knows what the outcome's going to be."

I'm starting to think that I'm wasting my time.

A sign behind the bar flashes, "Raw egg in beer."

"Get ready. It's cock-a-doodle-doo time," Mimi announces.

"So is this a special ceremony for a special occasion?" I ask with a note of sarcasm.

"My seventy-nine-year-old mother does it everyday." Mimi says. "So do we. It's supposed to give you pep just when you think you're going to drop dead."

I can't pass up the chance. "Anyone plan on keeling over?"

A voice emerges from the crowd. "What are you here for anyway?"

"You all know why. I'm Daria Fante, and I'm here to do a story on the mayor. Do you believe he's going to die like he says he is, and if you love him so much, why doesn't anyone care enough to say something?"

"That's none of your business, Miss Fante," Al says.

"He called the paper!"

The room grows quiet. Finally, the mayor breaks the silence. "I say we buy this woman a beer."

Everyone in the bar applauds as Gregory fills a mug and hands it to me, without a raw egg, I'm happy to see. The thought of gulping one of those down clots my throat the way watching my mother swallow raw clams on the half shell does.

"Mr. Mayor," I say nervously. "Thanks for the drink, but I came here for some answers."

"You'll get 'em. Now Greg, serve up the raw egg in beer, would ya?"

Gregory reaches into the refrigerator and hands a basket to the mayor. When the Christmas lights flash on, it's as though a mountain of eggs magically appears. Each alternates between shining like marble and returning to a dim shell with its unfinished flatness. Everyone jumps off their stools to form a line as they take turns getting an egg from the mayor. He hands one to all the patrons in the bar except me. I stay put in my seat.

Somehow, everyone keeps pace with the cadence of the lights. When the mayor hands them an egg, their faces glow and then vanish until the next person steps up. They return to their places one by one and wait for the mayor to take an egg from the basket and crack it on the rim of his glass.

When they hear the fragile sound, it's as though a bell goes off. They all crack their egg in a mug of beer and turn to face him. The mayor raises his glass high above his head and gazes at it the way a priest does a chalice before he drinks the blood of Christ. Everyone raises their glass in the air at the same time.

"Cock-a-doodle-doo," the mayor crows.

"Cock-a-doodle-doo," they crow back, repeating his words and intonation before chugging the egg and beer concoction.

An all-out procession follows. The mayor leaps off his stool and begins flapping his arms and waddling his rear end and turning his feet out. With the help of a disco ball hanging from the ceiling and flashing lights, colorful spots cover his body as his feathery moves turn into a slow-motion dance. Everyone forms a circle around the mayor and follows him as if he were doing some prescribed step like the polka or the hokey-pokey.

I ask Gregory, why the raw egg.

"We've been doing it every day for years," he says.

"Whose idea was it?"

"Who do you think? Sal's."

"How'd he do that? You couldn't get me to swallow one of those."

Gregory pounds on the counter to get everyone's attention. "Hey, Sal, I think you better tell this reporter a little story. You know the one."

The mayor walks over to me and says, "Have another beer on me with . . ."

"Without the raw egg, thank you."

He sits down in the stool next to me and closes my reporter's notebook. "Let me tell you something to put in your story. My papa, Francesco Antonio Taviani, was a coal miner. And when he crawled out of that big black hole in the earth at the end of the day, his lungs were so full of coal dust, there was no room left for air. He rested his hand on his chest and wheezed and snorted and gasped just to push and pull every breath he'd take. He might as well have been playing the accordion."

"When my mama heard her old man coughing outside the door, she greeted him by handing him a hose to wash off in the courtyard where the hens wandered from the coop after laying eggs. As he was hosing himself down, a stray hen squatted and laid an egg right smack in the middle of a steaming puddle of soot. That egg was as white as that puddle was black. He couldn't believe that a hen would lay an egg on a bed of wet coal dust and took it for a miracle."

The mayor stops to down the rest of his beer.

"Now my papa slipped the egg in his pocket and sat at the supper table. Grime was still caked under his fingernails even after a good scrubbing to clean it out, which made Mama upset when she saw his ten stubby mineshafts grabbing for a white napkin."

"Papa said, 'That dirt is deeper than the coal. I can't get that out.'"

"'You dig out the coal, every last ounce of it, don't ya?' she reminded him."

"'That's cause we're buried alive down there, for Christ's sake.' The egg in his pocket cracked as he shifted in his seat."

"'Not if you were the mailman.' See, she always wanted him to work in a clean office and handle white envelopes."

"'You don't want me licking stamps all day getting dry in the mouth. 'Least now I can come home and kiss ya.'"

"Normally after dinner, he'd drop off on the couch with the newspaper on his chest, but that day he pulled out the egg and finished cracking it in a glass of beer and swallowed it. He felt the yolk slide down his throat and land in his stomach. Not long after that, feathers started growing inside. He knew because they tickled him so much he squirmed until he fell off the couch and started to roll on the floor and scratch his belly. The missus grabbed a broom and started beating him with it because she thought he had some kind of varmint crawling inside his britches. That's when my papa got up and did a jig around the room with Mama hanging over his shoulder like a sack of potatoes. All of a sudden, he had so much life in him, he flew to the rooftop and crooned at the top of his lungs one long note that seemed to last forever and ever to make up for all the air sucked out of him little by little with every short, inner tube gasp and crankshaft cough and pickled snort and karate chop hack and whistling wheezing from working in a coal mine all those years of his life. He got his breath back."

The mayor puts his hand on my shoulder. "Now do you see why an egg?"

I nod as I look down at the blank page in my reporter's notebook.

"Why don't you write it down in your tablet?"

"I'll remember."

"What about getting the facts straight?"

"I'm not thinking about facts right now."

"Then let me ask the questions and you come up with some answers."

"It wouldn't be professional of me."

The mayor picks up my notebook, waves it above his head and throws it down. "Life ain't a profession, and faith ain't a science. And you can quote me on that." He looks for me to crack a smile. "What's the matter with you?"

"Your story made me remember one," I whisper.

"I'm listening."

I tell the mayor about my grandmother and how her boy drowned in the river one Easter. He and a buddy took their boat out early that morning, hoping to catch a few fish for Easter dinner. The water was high and choppy and their boat capsized. He was a good swimmer and could have made it to the bank, but he tried to save his friend. They went down together. The Coast Guard dragged a net to search for their bodies. Three days later, they found them in an embrace. My grandmother buried her son with an egg in his coffin and gave one to the other boy's mother. More than ever, she was a believer in the afterlife.

"You're a good Catholic girl, aren't ya?"

"I wish. You know what I used to do when I went to church? Sit in the balcony with my friend and count the bald heads. The organist told our Sunday school teacher and got us in trouble. I quit going to church years ago. My mom says if I walk in one now, the roof would cave in on me."

"The roof don't matter. It's what's inside of you that you don't want caving in."

The Christmas lights flash on and off and have the same calming effect on me as listening to myself breathe. "So you're going to keep on living?" I ask.

The mayor looks at the bottom of his glass.

"I mean after you die."

He looks up to the fan paddles, his eyes blinking with every rotation, and says, "There's a chicken inside me, ain't there?"

"One in you and one in everybody here."

"Except you," he says. "Why?"

Just then the chatter in the bar stops as if everyone senses what we're talking about. But they kept on fidgeting to fill the hole of silence. Gregory circles his sponge in the same spot on the counter. Rita keeps trying to shape the lily up the way she would a wilted curl. Mimi folds her lips until they disappear from her face. Rich races his finger around the rim of his glass. Ed lifts his baseball hat off his head and tucks his hair under it. Al fingers his zipper until it gets stuck halfway as he drops his hands and begins sniffing away his tears while he speaks. "You ain't gonna hatch here no more."

The mayor humors him. "Don't you worry, I'll keep the coop warm for ya. You know I will as sure as I'm sitting here. Now raise your glass for a toast. I believe . . . correction. I know for a fact this young lady here is ready to have her first cock-a-doodle-doo. And she's gonna have it here with us."

"I appreciate it but . . ."

The mayor reaches for an egg in the basket and offers it to me. "What would your nonna do if she were here?"

I take the egg from the mayor and hold it for a moment before I hand it back to him. Our eyes meet and he grins as he cracks it in my glass of beer and I watch the yolk float on the foamy surface like a life preserver on a wave. Everyone raises their mugs. I slowly open my mouth and then tip the glass 'til a flood roars down my throat. I squirm. I waddle. I flap. I fly. I crow. I do my best imitation of the mayor's chicken imitation all the way out the door. The mayor leads everyone in the bar out to the parking lot to escort me—chicken style—to my car. My instinct is to wave good-bye, but I don't. I flap instead and the mayor flaps back.

On the drive home, I'm still flapping and crowing. Once I get to bed, I can't fall asleep. I kick off my covers. I move from side to side, front to back. I feel the feathers in my pillow scratch my cheek. I get up, ready to dial the hospital to see if the mayor was admitted but drop the phone on the receiver. I tell myself I came to believe at the bar. Why wouldn't I now?

I plop back down on my feather pillow. I notice it feels softer on my cheeks now. I still can't fall asleep but not because I have doubts. I know what I believe is true, and I don't want to let go of that feeling, the power of not needing proof. The mayor is dead, and he left everyone at the bar last night with more than a chicken dance.

I wait until sunrise to get dressed. Even though I don't have the 6:00 A.M. shift, I get to work early. I don't take my coat off or set my briefcase on my desk. I head straight to my editor who has undoubtedly checked with the coroner to verify his death.

"You've got a story to write, Daria. He died in his sleep after attending a special council meeting on stop sign installations. The coroner couldn't find a thing wrong with him. Had no choice but to say the cause of death was old age."

I tell her I already knew.

"How? Did you call the coroner?"

"I have my source," I say as I sit down at my computer and begin leafing through each page of my reporter's notebook as if it were the

Bible. When I get to the section on Major's Tavern, I put one hand on the cold keyboard to type up my story. I lay the other on my warm stomach where I can still feel a tickle.

Shelf Life

S he was walking down the crooked porch steps, her purple
straw hat floating above the thicket of Jerusalem artichokes
in the front yard until her body reemerged at the sidewalk
where she waited for me to pass.

"Do you eat cereal?" she asked.

Her question jolted me as much as the two Scotties and beagle I
walked everyday. I halfheartedly tugged at their leashes, but the dogs
were too revved up to stop. Mac made strangled, gagging noises as
he lunged with his jaw to bite a mouthful of air as if it were a jumbo
sandwich. Tosh was jumping up on her hind legs, her front paws
occasionally landing on Mac's back, wagging her tail as steadily as a
windshield wiper. Lucy was marching quickly along with her spotted coat that resembled army fatigues while her ears hung over her
face like the flaps of an untied aviator's cap.

The three dogs combined almost weighed as much as I did. In
fact, when their owner, Brad, looked at how thin I was, he asked if
I would be able to handle them. He knew that standing still they
may be eighty-seven pounds of fat but on the run, they were two
hundred pounds of energy.

I didn't feel like stopping either.

"Sometimes," I called, glancing back at the woman.

"What kind?" she shouted.

By this time, I was halfway down the street and didn't want to say I ate granola from the bulk bin of the East End Food Co-op. I was told this block was a Shredded Wheat stronghold since some of the people still had jobs at the Nabisco plant. Eating another brand of cereal in this Pittsburgh neighborhood was as bad as driving a Toyota in the days when our steel mills were running.

The dogs stopped to sniff, so I turned to take a better look at this woman's house. It wasn't painted up like the ones on the hill or covered with aluminum siding like the ones on the flat. The wood was stripped down.

I grew up thinking it was good that people had to cover their homes with dark siding or shingles so soot from the mill didn't show. It meant people were working, and nobody cared if they couldn't paint a house a pretty color because all it did was turn gray anyway. Now that the mills were mostly closed down, some people who could afford it were hiring color consultants to paint their house with a half dozen colorful shades like the Victorians in San Francisco. That's what Lucy, Mac, and Tosh's owner, Brad, did.

Then my eye spotted the one bright thing about this woman's house, a lemon yellow pulley, bouncing with light. It was the same putrid color of the Jell-O salad my mother used to make with carrots and pineapple. One line of the pulley led from her attic window to the garage and another to a big dumpster. It looked like it belonged in a circus act—all it needed was an acrobat swinging from it. When I began walking the dogs a few weeks ago, Brad had warned me to look out for a woman with a fluorescent pulley.

"Her name's Olive LaRosa and she carries a weapon," he told me.

"A weapon?" It seemed a bit melodramatic.

"Well, I've never seen it, but she wears a holster. She hums all the time too."

"So?"

"She's a couple of megabites short of a hard drive. Needs some recircuiting upstairs. And if you stop to talk to her, I guarantee no matter what you say, it'll all come back to cereal. Trust me."

"I can think of worse things to talk about. At least in some circles."

"And she had the nerve to buy a set of dishes at the church garage sale and then try and sell them to me for twenty dollars more. Can you believe that?"

Brad was looking for sympathy, but he wasn't going to get any from me. If he wasn't paying me to walk his dogs, I would have asked if it occurred to him that Olive may not have a lot of money. Not everyone made the transition to a high-tech job like he did when he became a computer programmer. Most workers I knew went from production line to soup kitchen line.

"Between you and me, I don't know what she does with her money. She sure doesn't put it in the upkeep of her house. She won't even buy a can of oil for that pulley of hers."

I didn't know what it sounded like, but I had to admit as the dogs continued to sniff out what looked to be an ice cream spill, I was getting a headache from looking at it.

Olive appeared again from behind her screen door, still wearing her purple straw hat and carrying a bowl. She sat down on her porch swing and hummed between bites. When she drank from the bowl, I thought she might be eating cereal. She went inside, but reappeared out her attic window to drop something into a box she hooked on her pulley. When she set it in motion, it sounded as if the sky were the mouth of a squealing pig.

Lucy was the first to react as she lifted her tail and head and began crooning nonstop. She was clearly the melody, but two harmonizers were beside her, ready to join in. Mac and Tosh delivered short, punchy notes, repeating themselves like backup singers. Lucy's howl was tremulous with feeling. It moved up and down the scale, her high registers as impressive as her low ones.

My ears were about to pop. Now I could see as well as hear why her neighbors complained to Brad, who was president of the neighborhood watch. When the noise stopped, I managed to maneuver the dogs back to the front of her house and tried to be polite.

"You may have heard this before, but that pulley of yours . . ."

"It's not noise. It's opera." Olive shouted down, adjusting her hat. "It has perfect pitch, too. That's why I won't oil it."

Even at high volume, Olive talked in a slow expressionless monotone. It sounded as though I could run around the block and back and she'd still be on the same syllable. What could she possibly know about perfect pitch?

I walked up the stairs a little ways. "Well, you might want to reconsider before the neighbors make you take it down. You know there's a complaint filed against you."

"They're jealous," she said.

"Of what?"

"People say they can see my pulley past the railroad tracks, past the post office, and clean up to the funeral home. You know why they can see my pulley that far away? Because it's our very own North Star."

"And what else is in your house? Three kings bearing gifts of gold, frankincense, and myrrh?" I thought she might be offended by my sarcasm but she seemed glad just to talk.

"For your information, I run a business inside. What you're looking at is tax-deductible, operational equipment."

"So no baby Jesus bundled in a Styrofoam box in the broom closet?"

I was expecting her to get angry and drop a brick on my head or something, but she did something I never would have thought: she laughed.

"I've been accused of many things, but not that." She tipped her hat to me. "It doesn't surprise me, though. Nobody's bothered to come inside to see what I really do in here. That's all I'm asking. I'd be happy to work with them."

"So you have your own business. What do you do? I work for myself too. I'm a critter sitter." I didn't tell Olive, but my parents called me a quitter sitter. They thought a college graduate with an associate's degree had no business walking dogs for a living. I would humor them and say that I read Marx and Hegel to the dogs as I walked them, but they weren't amused. They thought I was wasting my time and said so. If I were motivated, I'd find an office job with benefits and a furnished apartment regardless of how bad the economy was.

"Want to come see?"

"Thanks, but I really should walk these dogs."

"See. You're just like them," she said, pulling her head in from the window.

I hesitated, then impulsively yelled, "I do eat cereal!"

She poked her head back out. "You do?" Her tone fluctuated before she returned to her monotone. "What kind?"

"Granola. Mostly."

"Boxed or unboxed?"

"I buy it in bulk."

"Boxed or unboxed?"

"I better go. The dogs are getting restless."

She held up her pointer finger, then disappeared. A few seconds later, she dropped three strips of rawhide from the window. Mac, Tosh, and Lucy charged up to them and began chewing.

"That should keep them busy for a few more minutes," she called down. "Boxed or unboxed?"

"In a bag. Unboxed."

"Oh." Olive shoved as much disappointment as she could into that two-letter word. "I was hoping you'd say you ate the variety snack packs. Do you know anyone who eats variety snack packs?"

"What kind?"

"General Mills."

"I don't think so. Why?"

"Then you can't help me." She looked down at something, probably a list. "What about Lucky Charms? I have nothing to cut today."

"With a knife, you mean?"

"Can't skin something that stiff any other way. It's like rawhide."

I braced myself. "Just what are you cutting?"

"I need proof," Olive said.

"Of what?"

"Proof of purchase labels," she said impatiently.

"You collect empty boxes?"

"They're not empty. If I get enough, I can have a full one all over again."

"So you skin boxes with a deadly weapon?"

"I'll only trade full value. No half buys," she said.

"I don't know what you're talking about."

"I'll show you what I have."

I glanced over at the dogs. They were sitting in the grass, gnawing away at their treats.

"You can bring them in," she said.

My curiosity got the best of me. I had to see just what kind of an operation an armed woman obsessed with cereal boxes who rigged a few ropes on a pulley and called it business equipment had. If she supported herself, who was I to judge? And I'd tell Brad if he didn't kill me first for bringing the dogs here. That part he wouldn't have to know.

"Just for a minute."

I led the dogs to the door, each with a rawhide between their teeth. Olive was there, holding the screen door open for us. I couldn't help but notice that she wore calluses on her fingers like some people wore diamond rings. My first thought was if a woman is this determined to collect cereal boxtops, why can't she find a real job? But I knew the answer to that. There weren't very many. That's one reason why I was walking dogs for a living. And there was one good thing about self-employment: no bosses.

After three office jobs and three bad bosses in a row since I graduated from community college, I liked the sound of that. There was Mr. Gargerring, the publicist who peaked years ago when he designed a coloring book of big wheelers for a trucking association. He had a habit of disappearing before press conferences. Once I searched the building for a half hour before I found him sitting in the corner of an empty boardroom munching on a bag of cheese puffs, which certainly explained where the orange fingerprints on the press releases came from. Then there was Malcolm, the insurance salesman who spent his afternoons cleaning the wax out of his ears with paper clips while I collated policies. No wonder I insisted on using the stapler. The worst was Bernie, who managed an appliance store. He showed me how to record inventory by grabbing the pencil out of my hand and bearing down so hard, he broke the point. It got so I didn't bother sharpening them anymore because I refused to see another one snap from the pressure. I let them get good and dull. As much as I needed work to meet people and socialize, I realized I'd rather be with friendly dogs than unfriendly people.

"My name's Nadine, by the way."

"I'm Olive. Let me walk you through."

"Now that I know you have a sense of humor, can I tell you what your pulley reminds me of?"

"The aria of an opera?"

"A tightrope, actually."

"A tightrope!" Olive exclaimed. She seemed satisfied with this and was patting Lucy so close to her eyes that the dog opened and shut them with each stroke.

"See, I had this vision as I was looking up at it. All my old bosses are part of a flying trapeze act. Lucy and Mac and Tosh here are up on their hind legs cracking long whips. I can see my first boss, Mr. Gargerring, riding a brand new dump truck across the tight rope. It's loaded with the cheese puffs he likes so much. He tosses them so lovingly out to the crowd, puff by puff, and everyone's hands are held above their heads ready to catch one as if it were money. But when they discover it's just junk food, they whip them back up at him. My second boss, Malcolm, is dressed in a tuxedo made of paperclips— even the bowtie, his top hat, and cane. All paperclips. He soft shoes along the rope until a giant horseshoe magnet appears. He tries to escape, but the attraction is too strong. Next, my third and last boss, Bernie, comes out on the rope dressed in striped tights, balancing a sharpened pencil the size of a sword on his nose. Meanwhile the dogs take their bows and get all the applause."

"Sounds like you either hate your bosses or love dogs," Olive concluded.

"I never hated my bosses. They just didn't understand me."

"And dogs do?"

"Better than anybody else I know."

"Not even friends?"

"Dogs are friends. When I was a kid, I wanted to take our dog, Leroy, to be my partner on our school trip to Kennywood Park so we could go on the rides together. My classmates were all paired up, but Leroy would have been my first pick anyway. My other choice was to ride with our principal, Sister Mary Alberta. She was looking for a skinny kid to sit with since she was on the heavy side. I was the skinniest, but I decided to stay home rather than have her habit blow in my face the whole time. And when Bernie fired me, I took my own dog for the longest walk. I had to put her to sleep last year," I added sadly.

"Don't you have any people friends?"

"Sure I do. But they're all getting married and planning their weddings with their fiancés."

"That doesn't mean they have a friend either. I was married once."

I stooped down to pet the dogs and asked what happened.

Olive shook her head before she spoke. "What he collected I thought was junk, and what I collected he thought was junk."

I took a look around her house. "I could see where that would be a problem for you, Olive." That was kind of like me and my parents, I thought to myself. They want to buy me a matching bedroom set because they can't understand how I can sleep on a matress on the floor of my studio apartment and use an upside down fruit crate for a nightstand. But when I looked at the fake wood coating and plastic handles of the furniture set they could afford to buy me, I decided I liked mine better.

"I don't miss him. But I miss having a partner."

"You should see Mac when Tosh isn't around," I said. "He gets all grumpy. He growls at everything in sight, even his bone. And Tosh. When Mac's not around, she'll look everywhere for him, whining. When they're reunited, they walk together like a marching band, side by side, their noses perfectly even. It makes Lucy here envious. It makes me envious for that matter."

I changed the subject. "So let's talk business. Show me what you've got."

Instead of curtains, Olive used clothes to cover some of her windows. She had them rigged cleverly with a pair of pants in the middle so that if she wanted to let light in, she could spread the legs apart. I noticed she had a belt around her waist with a small leather holder for her knife. She wore a red tank top and stretch shorts. I thought she'd take her purple straw hat off in the house but she didn't. She took off her brown saddle shoes, though.

Her dining room was a limbo for hundreds of empty bottles that seemed to float above the bulky pieces of dark wood furniture so permanently in their places. My eye stopped dead before the massive blocks of mahogany, and yet it glided through the transparent bottles as if there were no boundaries. In this room, there were thick orange curtains with a rubbery lining that kept the sun out except where the ends didn't meet. From that opening, the sunlight shone on a glass bottle as though a single votive candle were lit in the room. Other bottles were scattered on the table. They occupied chairs, stretched across a huge buffet server, and were kept in a china closet.

Olive carried a box of them into her bathroom and dropped them into a running tub one by one, sprinkling water on each as though she were baptizing a baby. When the label came off, she took the bottle out and gently dabbed it with a washcloth.

"Next I alphabetize the labels," Olive explained, leading the way to the living room.

On one of the walls, instead of paintings, she had hung a long strip of colorful fabric with rows of clear plastic pockets stuffed with proof of purchase labels showing through. The pattern of black lines from pocket to pocket was a long message in secret code. I was sure they formed symbols, and the symbols formed words that told a story with beginnings and endings. I didn't understand but I imagined Olive was the only one who did.

Olive had conventional furniture in this room as well, but it too was sacrificed for the cause. She turned lampshades upside down on coffee tables and filled them like baskets. Corners of lumpy pillows on the green sofa were barely visible under piles of boxtops. The dogs weren't even tempted to jump up. The floor was a mosaic pathway of labels that led upstairs.

In the hallway, my leg scraped up against a bushel basket filled with Styrofoam peanuts that Lucy sniffed out.

"Sure there's no baby Jesus buried in there somewhere?" I teased Olive.

"I refill my bean bag chairs with those. Could you use some?" Olive explained that she got them for free in the parking lot of a shipping warehouse. I told her, no thanks.

In the next room, there was a netless ping pong table in the center surrounded by flattened boxes of all sizes, little boxes of cereal snack packs and big boxes of washing machine detergent. Lucy plopped herself on one. Mac and Tosh followed.

"I make the first cut here. Doesn't matter what shape or size. I do the same thing for each one of my boxes," Olive said, pointing to a crease on the box. "Then I spread them out. After they're flat, I stack them so the proof of purchase label is on the top right corner. Next, I gut them."

"Gut them?"

"Take out the proof."

"You were right, Olive. This is quite an operation."

"After that, I check for bonus tops, skin those and send the remains to the dumpster. I need to get fifty done a day to make a living."

"You mean to say you live off of coupons and proof of purchase labels?"

"Hunt 'em down daily. I've been doing it for twenty-six years, Nadine."

Olive said she went to all the conventions for trading coupons and labels. At the last one, she said, she picked up a few leads for variety snack packs and one for Lucky Charms, but they fell through.

"Everybody's holding on to them right now. Cash rebate. Can't pass that up. Especially when you've got debts to pay to someone who doesn't barter. Deadbeats." She frowned and picked up the steak knife from the ping pong table. "Most people take these boxes for done and just bury them in the trash. I give them more than a shelf life."

Olive cut out a round label the size of a half dollar and showed it to me on the point of her knife. I indulged her by looking closely. "As good as hard, cold cash. How did you start collecting all of this anyway?"

"My husband was laid off from his job. I knew he wouldn't get it back, and I knew he wouldn't get another one because there was no place for him to go. I started with little things. Like packets of sugar and salt and creamers from the Eat N' Park. Then one day I realized I shouldn't be going after things that were full but empty containers. They're what's left behind. I knew they had another life in them nobody else could see. You do see, don't you?"

"Olive, either a box is empty or full. That's how I see it."

"Still, you can help me collect labels when you walk the dogs if you want to. I noticed you take them in the alley past the garbage cans," she said.

"You want me to pick through . . ."

"Not you, Lucy. Beagles have a keen sense of smell. We could train her. All you have to do is mark the cans."

"I know you like Lucy and see she's a good dog, but I don't think her owner would go for that. In fact, I know he wouldn't."

"I'd really appreciate it. I need to keep up with my quota."

"Then why don't you own a beagle?"

"I have to keep my overhead low."

I started toward the doorway. The dogs didn't move from their cardboard nests.

"You know who owns these dogs, don't you? The president of the neighborhood watch."

"They want to kill my business," Olive blurted out.

"Because they don't know you make a living doing this. If you got rid of the pulley's noise with a can of oil and covered the flashy yellow with electric tape, they'd leave you alone. Write it off as an improvement."

We walked back to the front door. Olive apologized for asking me to help and insisted I have a snack with her before I left. "I'll play you a song."

"Let me guess. Your favorite band is the Boxtops."

Olive smiled. "It should be, but I was thinking of opera. It'll just take me a minute to find the albums. Oh, and I forgot a new needle for the record player."

"Please, don't bother."

"Sure about that, Nadine? It won't take me as long as it looks."

"Thanks. Maybe some other time."

In the kitchen, I watched her wash squares of used aluminum foil and hang them out to dry with clothespins. Then she opened up a refrigerator filled with paper plates. She deliberately moved them back and forth, rearranging them like checkers. Finally, she pulled out a square of cheese and cut mold off.

"I found this in the trash pile. I knew it was still good inside," she said. "It's provolone."

Olive told me she takes home all the leftovers from potluck parties because she offers to be the cleanup crew. She said she goes to a church party once a week. She spread out a plastic tablecloth, trying to flatten the wrinkles, and on navy blue party napkins with matching Dixie cups, we ate cheese on stale crackers and drank flat cherry pop. The dogs chomped on biscuits. Eventually Olive brought out a tin of cookies. We got talking about ingredients, and I mentioned in passing that my aunt only uses the whites of eggs when she bakes.

"What does she do with the yolks?"

"She throws them out."

"That's a shame," she said, drawing out her syllables even more than she normally did. The way she looked at me, you'd think I'd told her my mother made a habit of dropping diamonds in the garbage disposal.

I explained that my aunt lived in another state to avoid any hopes on Olive's part that I could somehow be a middle person in a yolk exchange. She nibbled on her cookie much more slowly after that, as if she were plotting a way to rescue those yolks.

Olive didn't say anything more about getting the dogs to sniff out cereal boxtops. She just thanked me for the visit. I reminded her about getting a can of oil and electric tape for the pulley ASAP if she wanted the neighbors to drop the complaint. She said she would as soon as she had the money to buy them. She needed to trade in some labels and coupons first.

"I'd be happy to buy them for you if you want."

"Thanks, but you don't have to do that."

The thought of her not being able to afford these seemed crazy to me at first, but then I thought back on the moldy cheese and church potlucks she relied on for food and how wasted egg yolks depressed her. It wasn't far fetched. Olive was a hunter and gatherer living from hand to mouth. People in her situation who weren't as industrious would be on welfare or on the street. I talked to Brad about it when I saw him the next morning. I told him I had seen and heard Olive's pulley.

"What did I tell you, Nadine? We've asked her politely to take that thing down, and she hasn't. The board met last night and voted to press charges."

"You can't do that! She makes her living using that pulley."

"Yes, we can and we will."

"What if she oils it and covers up the yellow?"

"She's got two days to do it. We're pressing charges the day after tomorrow. She's a public nuisance."

Olive was the anticonsumer. And like her neighbors thought, she was dangerous. They spent. She saved. They tossed out. She caught it in the air without even waiting for the first bounce. She believed in an afterlife. They didn't. As soon as Brad left for the office, I took the dogs for their morning walk to the hardware store for the oil and tape and then to Olive's. I handed them to her as soon as she opened the door.

"Here. You have two days to fix that pulley or the police will come."

"I don't believe it! They called the police?"

Lucy snuck in and began sniffing an empty box of Lucky Charms that Olive had in the hallway.

"Lucy, get back here!"

She came to the door with her snout stuck in the box. She started moving backwards from the box, but it followed her. She shook her head and finally it dropped off. Meanwhile, Mac was tearing across the porch with a box he'd been chewing on while Tosh was pawing and licking hers, and all the while, I was trying to untangle their leashes.

"You better get working on that pulley," I said.

"But I can't pay you right now."

"Don't worry about it, Olive. I gotta go."

Our walk started out like it always did—the dogs vying for their positions. Then Lucy must've gotten a whiff of something and we were off. She charged a garbage can. I tried to stop her, but Mac and Tosh helped her tip it over. It rolled down the alley a ways before crashing into a birdbath filled with pigeons. They flapped their wings in a frenzy and caught Mac's eye. He chased them for a half a block before he gave up, all the while pulling me in tow. That's when he started snapping at Tosh's ear like a sore loser. And Tosh snapped back.

A car pulled out of a garage and backed into a mud puddle, which splattered onto the entangled duo. I knelt down to wipe the mud off the dogs just when Lucy got wind of a smell from the garbage can they had just knocked over. Lucy's leash pulled me one way, Mac's and Tosh's the other. I was caught in the middle of a tug of war. It was a deadlock until Tosh defected to Lucy's side and I was dragged into the mud puddle. I now had one white shoe, one brown, and a twisted ankle.

"Lucy! Mac and Tosh! HEEL!" I yelled.

The dogs chewed and fought over pieces of garbage that had spilled out of the can. Mac furiously shook a cereal box in his jaws until it flew from his mouth and landed near a neighbor's doghouse. Lucy ran after it.

"Lucy, COME HERE!" I yanked at her leash but Mac and Tosh were already following her. No sooner did they reach the cereal box than a Doberman sprung from the doghouse and growled. They yelped and fled and now the leashes were a rope and I was being towed. I stepped on the cereal box and tried to get my footing with my good ankle, but suddenly I was skiing on it with one leg, riding on their determination through the alley. I knew I couldn't let go. We sped through the alley, veering toward a brick wall. All I remember for sure was that the mortar between the bricks was grit between my teeth.

Who knows how much time passed, but I awoke feeling a vibration. Something underneath gently rumbled the way a car does up and down the grooves in the road. There seemed to be an echo. I couldn't make out the words—if they were words or a mumbling tone.

"Nadine? Are you awake?"

Still dizzy, I looked around to see where I was as if that would help me answer the question. It turned out I was lying on Olive's couch between two lampshades.

"You don't remember, do you?"

I lifted my head an inch off the pillow and had to put it back down. "Where are the dogs?"

Olive patted me on the shoulder. "They're back now. It's five o'clock."

"Where'd they go?"

"For a run."

I put my hands on my forehead and felt a damp cloth there. "Wasn't I with them?"

"Part of the way."

"The leashes. I didn't let go."

"Brad wants to see you. You hit a brick wall and the dogs got loose."

"Oh no." I tried sitting up, but Olive guided me back down.

"They're fine," Olive assured me. "Lucy came to my door, and I took them all home. But I brought you back here in my wagon. You had enough for one day."

Olive said she gave me a massage because I hit my shoulder and was dragged a ways. My ankle was swollen too.

"I know this isn't my business, but I think the dogs are too much for you."

"Two hundred pounds of energy," I mumbled under my breath.

She propped up my pillow and handed me a box. The lid was gift wrapped with a loosely curled yellow ribbon.

"Open it for me."

Between tissue paper, which had long lost its crispness, was a packet of coupons. She took them out and showed me. One was for a free dinner for two and the others were for free boxes of granola and dog treats. Olive said she got them by sending in proof of purchase labels.

"I'm really sorry, Nadine. I was hoping I could at least buy you dinner."

She took out a slip of paper with names and gave it to me.

"What's this?"

"People I know from church who have dogs and cats. Maybe they need your services."

She closed the tissue paper and put the lid back on the box, which she had used many times before and would no doubt use many times after. I knew that with Olive it wouldn't be empty for long.

Freezer Burn

Sophia takes one look at the ball of our Sicilian great grand-mother's starter dough she pulls out of the freezer and mumbles two words: freezer burn. I know my sister will blame me if we can't get it to rise.

"I thought you were the gourmet cook around here, Charlene."

"I wrapped it in foil *and* plastic wrap. Besides, peasant bread is hardly gourmet."

"It may not look like it, but this is our family heirloom," Sophia says, waving the dough in my face. "This is what we have from Sicily. No diamonds to pass on from generation to generation. We have a graying lump of dough. This is our forever!"

"Then why did you wait forever to use it! I told you you shouldn't have left it in the freezer for so long!"

I take it and watch it sparkle from all the crystals of ice that have grown on its surface despite my careful wrapping. I hold it above Sophia's ring finger and tell her our rock is highly refractive, but my sister isn't amused.

"We promised Mom we'd pass this on to another generation. It's up to us."

She begins chipping away at the coat of ice on the starter dough with a potato peeler as slowly as I imagine one chips away at finger-nail polish. That's my sister being the idealist that she is. Maybe that's why she still goes to church and I'm the jaded lapsed Catholic who stopped believing.

"No. *You* promised Mom. Besides, we have to have children before we can pass it on, Sophia, and you know I don't want any."

She throws the peeler at me.

"Well, I do! So start chipping." She reaches in her pocket for a rubber band to tie her hair back in a ponytail and stretches it so much, it snaps.

"Don't forget, you're the one who begged for my help, Ms. Kitchen Catastrophe," I remind her as I take stabs at the ice. "You're the one whose idea of cooking is to wait for the smoke alarm to go off to know something's done. You're the one who cooked green beans until they looked like cigarette ashes in a pan welded on the electric burner—the equivalent of a Three Mile Island meltdown, I might add. Then there was the sonic boom when your boiling eggs exploded—shells splattered all over the place. You were lucky you didn't get hit in the eye with the shrapnel. Remember that?"

"Are you done yet?"

"And your third K.C. wasn't a charm. It was a warning the time the ceiling light fixture fell just after you walked out from under it. Good thing you didn't take the time to stir the linguini. No wonder you didn't complain about eating half-cooked clumps of pasta after that close call. In other words, there's a reason you need me. Unless this priest you invited to dinner has an iron stomach. Let's face it. If it weren't for me, you'd fill our shelves with boxes of Minute Rice and in that minute you'd find a way to ruin it."

Sophia puts on an apron and begins fumbling with the strings. "Do this for me, please," she begs.

"See, you can't even tie your own apron." I tug tightly before I make a bow.

"Okay, so I'm nervous."

"You have every reason to be."

Sophia takes the dough from me and begins melting away the Ice Age on it by running it through water so hot the steaming spigot looks like a dragon's nostril. "You know I've baked bread before with Aunt Josie?"

"Fantastic. Then you remember drafts are a no no. Would you get that for me?" I point to the window and wait for Sophia to close it.

"What does this revolve around?"

"Making bread, silly. And what kind of saying is that?"

"My global studies professor likes to use it. She even makes a circle with her finger."

"And now in my best imitation of Dad imitating Julia Child's voice, let me say that we're using wheat flour because it has more body than rye or corn as well as the fact that water and milk are the intriguers that lend steam to the performance. As for salt and sugar, they make essential but brief appearances, do they not? And finally, we know the yeast is what brings us the feast. Remember how Dad used to do that when he made pancakes on Saturday mornings?"

Sophia has a blank look on her face. I put my hands on my hips.

"Did your bread rise or not?"

"My loaf was the consistency of a brick," she admits. "But Aunt Josie made the best bread using this starter dough. She even shaped it. Remember? Crosses for Lent. Baskets at Easter time. Wreaths at Christmas."

"I was too young."

"You remember her *sfingies,* don't you? How we dipped them in molasses?"

"All I remember is Mom yelling at me for having sticky fingers the rest of the day."

"Figures."

I examine the frozen blob. It doesn't look promising. I suggest that we scrap the ethnic dough thing, and I make her professor a real meal. "How does salmon baked in parchment paper with lemon and dill, served with white butter and basmati rice with spinach, garlic, and shallots sound to you?

"Great but we can't do it."

"Okay, how about shrimp cooked scampi style with a goat cheese and herb timbale over greens with roasted red peppers, capers, and toasted pine nuts?"

"Charlene, no."

"I thought you needed to impress this guy. He's your thesis advisor, isn't he?"

"Yes, and he's the one who'll decide if I get the travel fellowship or not."

"All the more reason then," I say, reaching for my recipe box. "I've got a great recipe for pork chops stuffed with apples and mint. This, in your words, revolves around serving a good meal."

"Stop! I mentioned the starter dough in my application. Father Van Heuck loved it. He said it demonstrated my passion to go back and research family traditions. I even said I'd be serving it tonight."

"So what you're saying is this dough means . . . dough?"

"You'll get it to rise, won't you?" she pleads.

"Sophia, no offense, but we'll be wasting our time if we try to bake this. We'll need a chainsaw to cut it. You want to take that risk?"

"Going back may mean nothing to you, Charlene, but I promised Mom I'd keep this dough in the family. I've always dreamed of bringing it back to Castroreale the way Nonna brought it here."

"Know what I promised Mom? That I'd never make her eat Meals on Wheels for as long as she lived."

"Charlene, please!" Her eyes are glistening.

"All right. What time's Father Van Heuck coming for dinner?"

"Seven o'clock."

"We better hurry then because I want to stuff it with some veggies and cheese." I defrost the starter dough, combine it with a new batch I mix up, cover the dough with a cloth, and sprinkle some flour on a board for kneading.

Sophia rolls up her sleeves, takes off her birthstone ring, and touches the dough as if she were playing the piano for the first time.

"Use the palm of your hand and fold the dough over toward you."

"I can't. It's sticking to my fingernails."

"Do it until the dough becomes smooth."

"Aren't you going to set a timer?"

"When we see air blisters, we're ready to put it in a bowl."

Sophia lifts the starter dough high in the air and flips it over, dusting our new toaster with flour so it looks like a car after a light snowfall.

"Sorry about that."

As I go get a damp cloth to sponge it off, she presses her palms into the dough as though she's trying to see if an imprint of her life line shows up.

"Sophia, this isn't play dough. You want it to rise, don't you?"

"I was just testing it."

"Put more of yourself into it. You should be using your whole body. Like this." I demonstrate kneading as if it were an exercise class, repeating the motion several times before letting her take over.

"Better. Now keep kneading," I tell her as I stare down at the starter dough. It still looks like a deflated beach ball, but I don't say anything.

"We're going to do it, Charlene. We're going to make this rise," she exclaims.

I look up at Sophia. With the exception of that starter dough, everything about my sister reaches out. She's got this personality that bubbles over and a petite body that seems to expand when she moves her hands, kind of like a card table when you unfold the legs. When she dries her hair, it's like a mountain of fluffy meringue grows on top of her head. She even wears a watch that pops out. Mickey Mouse in 3-D. And she's the kind of cook who doesn't make any recipe she can't double. She makes lasagna in a pan too big to fit in the oven. Her meatballs are the size of baseballs, and her birthday cakes are two whole cakes stacked one on top of the other so high that dinner forks shrink to miniatures. It would be endearing if you didn't have to eat any of it.

I give her further instructions, thinking if I weren't such a cynic, maybe I'd be able to look down at the starter dough and entertain the possibility of it rising. I force a smile as she gently rests the powdery glob on her chest like a baby, lowers it in a bowl, covers it with a towel, and then sets it in the oven on a rack over a pan of warm water.

"I'm sure you don't remember, but our great grandmother used to put her old fur coat on top of the bowl of dough to keep it warm enough to rise," Sophia explains.

"Don't get any ideas. A towel will do just fine."

"Now what?"

"We wait for it to double in size. Should take an hour and a half."

We take a break and go to our living room. The two swivel chairs we sit in are the only pieces of furniture besides a trunk and a hutch that the last tenant left because it was too heavy to move. Of course if Sophia had her way, the apartment would be cluttered with antiques.

"What direction should we face?" she asks cheerfully. "North and look out the windows to watch the traffic on Fifth Avenue?"

I shake my head.

"South and smell the ripe bananas in a basket on the hutch?"

"Pass."

"Well, then let's face each other and talk through the eucalyptus branches on the trunk between us."

"I got a better idea. Let's face the wall," I say, propping my bare feet on a poster hung with masking tape.

Charlene frowns.

"I'm a minimalist, what can I say?"

"Nonna told me once that the direction a chair faces in Castro-reale is very important. The men get to set up their chairs right outside the cafe and face the town square, so they can watch everyone while sipping out of tiny espresso cups they hold with big, stubby fingers. The women in town set up their chairs in the doorway of their homes since there are no porches. She said they face indoors and knit, feeling a breeze on their backs if nothing else."

"Is that in your fellowship essay? You could research the sociology of sitting."

"You mean instead of starter dough?" Sophia reproaches me.

"I didn't say that."

"That's what you're thinking, Charlene."

"Well, in case the dough doesn't . . ."

"Don't say it. Think positively for a change."

"I am," I argue. "You could take a new approach with Father Van Heuck. Put him in the swivel chair and tell him the same thing you told me."

When it's time, I signal for Sophia to check on the dough. She opens the oven door and lifts the towel. I'm surprised to see it actually rose a little. I put my finger in it to show her.

"See. My fingerprint stays in the dough. Very good sign."

I place the bowl on the counter and punch the dough down with a fist, work the edges to the center, and turn the bottom to the top, so Sophia can knead it some more. She stands on her tiptoes, as if she were wearing a pair of shoes with two-inch heels, and leans into the dough before she puts it back in the oven for a second rise. We go back to the living room.

"Rise, baby, rise," she chants as she raises her hands above her head.

Because the room is so bare, a result of my latest deconstructionist efforts to counter my sister's expansionist impulses, it has an echo. Sophia calls it a voice from on high offering back some of our words, the ones that are worth repeating. The ones that resonate. Sometimes she'll say words, just to hear them reverberate off the ceiling. She explained once it was her way of being inside the cavernous walls of a Gothic cathedral, looking up to see rows of round beams, wondering how long it will take for her words to touch bone.

"Come on, Charlene. Repeat after me!"

"I thought there was an echo to do that."

After a few minutes of saying the word "rise" over and over again, she gets up to walk back to the kitchen.

"It's not time."

"Can't we take a peek?"

"No way. A draft or even a loud noise could keep it from rising."

"How do we know when it's time?" she asks.

"About as long as it would take for you to go through that stack of old papers and get it down to yesterday's news. Now come on, let's kick back."

Eventually, we return to the kitchen and I give her more instructions for shaping loaves. Sophia dutifully follows through step by step.

Two round loaves—one big and one small—are covered with a cloth and resting, but Sophia is too excited to leave the room. We sit at the table and wait until it's time to put the loaves in the pan. "We're going to keep one of those for next time, right?"

"If we want to try and keep this thing going, yeah."

"Don't tell me the dough has to rise again!"

"You got that right."

Sophia wipes her greasy hands on her apron. "You mean to tell me after all this, it could still flop? Look how late it is. We don't have time to make something else if that happens, Charlene."

"Now who's the one that needs positive thinking? Go open a bottle of wine and chill. Your sis here is gonna take care of the rest."

When it's ready, or as ready as it's going to be, I take the small loaf and set it aside to wrap up later and store in the freezer. I stuff the big one with some veggies and cheese, brush it with fresh herbs and butter, put it in a big round bread pan, and then slide it in the oven. As soon as I walk into the living room, Sophia jumps out of her seat.

"I just remembered. We need to move the kitchen table in here."

"Why didn't you say so? We would have done it before I put the dough in the oven."

"Why? We have time."

"We have to be careful not to make too much noise."

While the dough bakes, we lift the kitchen table to move it into the living room, but it doesn't fit through the doorway. We hear the elevator's wooden gate close and its motor hum a note that gets higher and higher until it's cut off. The elastic elevator gate snaps back open.

Sophia panics. "Somebody just got off on our floor. What if it's him?"

"Turn the table on its side."

"I can't lift it that way! The wall's in the way."

"No. This way!"

We hear footsteps walking on the newspapers the super has put down in the hallway while he paints the ceiling.

Sophia opens the peephole to see. She runs back, covering her mouth. "Oh, my God. It's him. He's an hour early."

I try to stay calm.

"Quick. Lift it up!" She jiggles the corner of the table. "I can't. It's stuck."

We hear a knock on the door.

"Let's move it back into the kitchen."

"We can't, we'll disturb the dough. I'll get the door."

"Let's move this first!" Sophia turns her head to the door and yells, "Just a minute."

"Not so loud, Sophia. The dough."

We grab the table's cold metal legs by the ankles and turn it upside down, angling it through. We set it down on the throw rug in the middle of the living room. I hurry toward the door, but Sophia makes me wait another minute so she can cover the bare table.

Father Van Heuck's face reminds me of geometry. His goatee, a bunch of lines intersecting at a point just below his chin. His ears, perfectly round, about three-quarters of a circle. His nose, two sides of a right triangle, and his squarish cap with one side smashed in, a trapezoid. He is carrying what looks like a violin case.

"Come in. I'm Sophia's sister, Charlene."

"I hope I'm not too early," Father apologizes as he hands me a bottle of wine.

"Not at all." I roll my eyes once I turn my back to him. A white Catholic lie.

He follows me through the hallway. His scarf gets caught between the gears of my ten-speed bike stored in the corner. Father is jerked to a halt as he loosens the scarf's chokehold around his neck. I seat him in one of the swivel chairs and take his coat and violin case.

In the kitchen, Sophia and I check to make sure there are no bits of food between the prongs of the forks and no orange juice pulp on the glasses. I reach for the plates with the fewest scratches on the surface from the silverware.

"Something smells out of this world," Father says as I set the table. He waits until Sophia comes out from the kitchen and adds, "I bet your great grandmother has something to do with that!"

Sophia gives Father a big hug. "It should be ready in a bit," she says with a nervous giggle. Can I offer you a glass of wine?"

I signal for Sophia to sit next to Father. I fill their glasses and excuse myself. "If you don't mind, I'll bring the chairs in."

"You're welcome to join us, Charlene," Father insists.

"I'll be right with you." I carry two chairs from the kitchen and put them beside the table. I turn one to face them.

"Sophia was just about to tell me the history behind the starter dough."

Sophia rests her glass in the palm of her hand. "Well, it first rose from the yeast in our great grandmother's wooden bowl that our grandmother shipped over from Castroreale, their Sicilian hilltown. She said it was so hot in the boiler room of the ship where it rested for two and a half weeks, and the steady movement of the waves acted like a pair of hands kneading the dough from side to side. It doubled, then tripled in size until it popped off the lid on the bowl. It quadrupled, then quintupled in size and split open the barrel holding the bowl."

"Good heavens," Father says, sipping his wine.

Oh please, I think to myself. Raise the expectations, why don't you.

"Our grandmother filled a dozen mop buckets from the deck

with the starter dough at the end of the trip and earned her first dollar in America by selling loaves of bread. Each time she kept a small ball of the starter dough and added it to her next batch so it would always originate from the dough that rose from the yeast on the ship. She kept enough in her icebox to share with our mother, and before mother died, she gave a piece of the starter dough to us, her only daughters."

"What a compelling story," Father says before turning to me. "You must love to hear her tell it."

"It's the first time I've heard it, actually."

"Really?" He seems perplexed.

"I suppose I never bothered to ask."

Sophia runs her finger around her wine glass. "Charlene isn't as engrossed with our Sicilian heritage as I am."

"I see," Father nods.

"But now I'm really curious. Where did the recipe come from anyway, Sophia?"

"Why, that was my very next question," Father beams.

"The recipe is inspired by the wrath of the volcano, Mt. Etna. A little girl was on her way to Castroreale to buy her hungry family some grain. Halfway there, while crossing a stream, she lost the coin her mother gave her. She took off the shawl wrapped around her head and neck and cast it into the stream like a net, hoping to retrieve the coin. She fished for hours but only pebbles and driftwood were scooped into the shawl's web."

"It grew dark. She was about to give up and return home when the lip of Mt. Etna began to quiver. Soon it opened its mouth wide and spoke to her with words spewed out on a tongue of lava. The words flowed out but she couldn't hear the volcano in the distance so the tongue of lava followed her to get closer. Afraid, she ran to escape it. She looked back and saw that it was on her heels so she climbed a big rock along the stream. The lava stopped at the base of the rock.

"'Eat my words,' the volcano said to the girl, who sat still on the rock."

"'Eat my words. They will fill your hunger,' Mt. Etna repeated."

"'They are too hot to eat. I'll burn to my death if I swallow them.'"

"'They are frozen now. They will not burn.'"

"The girl reached for a twig to poke at the lava tongue, waiting for it to bubble and boil and melt the branch. The lava was solid. She felt the twig. It was frozen."

"'Eat my words. I speak for you,' the volcano said."

"The girl jumped off the rock and on the tip of the lava tongue was a white grainy substance, yeast powder from which the very first starter dough was made."

"'You will never run out again.'"

"'Never,' the girl said looking down at the handful of icy powder.'"

"'Never. As long as you divide this, it will multiply.'"

"The girl put the powder in her pocket and ran through the countryside back home. She told the volcano's instructions to her mother. 'If you divide this, it will multiply.'"

For the first time, I hear Sophia's words echo. She's always talking about how they flutter furiously above us like a caged bird that flaps from wall to wall, looking for an opening to fly out. But I always thought she was exaggerating.

"Sophia, you have such a gift for storytelling," Father remarks.

"She does, doesn't she?" I agree.

I pour us another glass of wine. Sophia had put hers down on the trunk when she began her story so she could use her hands to animate and hadn't touched it since.

"Charlene, maybe you could check in the kitchen."

"Oh, my. I was so busy listening to the story that I . . . If you'll excuse me, please."

I walk casually to the kitchen and then rush over to the oven. I peak through the window to check on the dough. It hasn't risen yet, but I'm hopeful because it hasn't fallen flat yet either. Any minute now, I say to myself. As soon as I return to the living room I smile and say, "It's just starting to brown. It'll be a bit longer."

Father turns to Sophia and says, "Why don't I play you a few songs before dinner? While we're waiting?"

"I saw the violin case! I didn't know you played an instrument, Father."

Privately, I worry that if it's too loud, it may affect the dough.

"Oh, I'd love to hear you, Father," Sophia chirps.

"I'm a little out of practice. I studied rather intensively for a couple of years, but just have time to play every now and then since chairing the fellowship committee."

"I'm sure you're wonderful. Please," she insists.

He goes to get his violin and music stand from his case as Charlene eagerly pulls out her chair to become his audience.

Father Van Heuck unfolds the portable stand and stands erect in front of it with his violin resting on his shoulder and his cheek resting on his violin. He pulls back the bow ready to begin when the sheet music abruptly closes. He creases the fold and takes his ready position once more as he holds the bow back even further this time, ready for a sweeping forward motion.

When his violin bow cuts across the strings, it sounds as though a sixty-nine-cent windshield wiper from G.C. Murphy is about to snap as it scrapes an icy surface.

"Piano, piano," I whisper to myself.

I sit on my hands and fidget to keep from covering my ears. Sophia folds hers and buries them in her lap. I just bet now she wishes the room didn't have an echo. Each note throws itself at the ceiling and explodes in our ears like a round of grenades. Each note, I'm convinced, pierces the dough, one pin prick after the other bursting a balloon. Then I think of the starter dough in a barrel and the steady movement of the waves. I begin to sway in my chair and somehow my mind goes back to my sister's stories. I hear each of her words instead of Father's violin.

In fact, I automatically clap at the end of one of Sophia's stories that I retold myself seconds before Father finishes his song.

Father picks up his windshield wiper, but Mickey emerges from

Sophia's wristwatch. She and I jump up from our chairs and excuse ourselves as Father finally puts his violin back in its case after his twenty-minute recital from hell.

"What sheer torture," Sophia giggles quietly. "Couldn't you have done something, Charlene? What about the dough?"

"It wasn't so bad after a while."

"What, are you deaf?"

"No, it's just that I started to think about you reciting those stories. I was with Nonna on that ship, Sophia! I heard the ocean waves! I heard the volcano talk to the little girl! You were marvelous! I'd give you the grant!"

"You're just saying that to brace me for what's behind that oven door," she says, handing me the potholders. Rather than open it, I look through the window but can't see anything because it's splattered with juice. "That's a good sign, Sophia." I hand her back the potholders and cheer her on. "Rise, baby, rise!"

"I can't look. You're the chef. Not me."

"If the dough rose on a ship, why not here?"

"It's gonna be flat. I just know it."

"Sophia, as if that isn't enough, you're forgetting something else. Every time you cook, the recipe's doubled. Hold that thought or you're going to have to eat your words. Remember your story."

I reach into the oven and slide out the bread. It's a puffy mound, steaming through a small opening at the top where the edges of the dough don't meet because it rose so much. It looks like a volcano just before an eruption. Sophia hugs me.

"Better than my Normandy soufflé!"

"I don't believe it. We made it rise!"

"Told you. Just like your story."

I seat Father and myself and let Sophia do the honors of carrying the dish into the living room. She sets it on the middle of the table and says as she serves it up. "Here it is. A dish made with my grandmother's starter dough."

Father eagerly spears a piece on his fork. Sophia and I wait for him to finish his first bite. "My compliments to the chef. I never thought it was possible for this to taste even better than it smells. And just look at it. Why it's practically risen to the heavens. I have no doubt your grandmother's spirit is with us now," Father smiles.

"I can hardly believe it," Sophia blurts out.

Father has a surprised look on his face. "You mean you didn't think it would?"

"Well, I . . ."

"She means it's a good thing we have high ceilings. Hope that's the case in Castroreale when Sophia gets there," I wink.

"Indeed," he says, puling out a newspaper clipping from his pocket. As he unfolds it, he explains that there was a volcanic eruption outside of Castroreale recently, on top of the earthquake that struck the area two years ago, which residents still hadn't recovered from. He says it wasn't cause to cancel Sophia's travel fellowship there but was all the more reason for her to go. More than ever, she'd be needed there. If she could cope with the devastation.

He hands her the piece of paper and warns her that it is not the idealized Castroreale she has in her mind. She shakes her head. I lean over to see it. It's a picture of a girl's feet sticking out of a mound of lava and stone under a Roman archway of a collapsed building.

She grabs my arm. "Oh my, look at that poor girl. And how many others?"

Father turns to Sophia. "I realize this is not the picture of Castroreale you probably had in your mind when you wrote your essay. Do you envision yourself still going? Coping with all the hardship you'll witness?"

Sophia swallows. "Yes, Father. I still want to go."

"As you see, this will not be just a trip about family roots. Much of the town is in ruins. I want to make sure that you can imagine yourself there now."

"I can," Sophia insists. "I can see it in my mind." Sophia closes her eyes and speaks as if she were in a trance. "The narrow alleyways where I'll lose my sense of direction until I spot Mt. Etna barely etched in a background haze and a blanket of golden patches spread out below it. I'll walk past buildings where all that's left standing is an archway or a corner or a wall with vines still clinging to it and a row of potted plants leaning against it. I'll pass two men standing on a pile of rocks, reaching toward the sky with their hammers and ask them where I can find the girl in the picture but will see they're concentrating on what must go up rather than what has come down."

"And what will you do to help?"

"In the café, I'll ask the bartender for directions. He'll shake his head, wipe his wet hands on a towel and write the directions in my journal. I'll thank him and when I get outside discover he just wrote the directions for making lemon ice probably because the recipe supposedly originated there and that's what Castroreale is known for."

"And then?"

"I'll head to the water fountain in the center of the town square and show three young girls dressed in pedal pushers and sandals the picture. One will point to a poster on the fountain wall announcing a funeral procession. I'll hurry to the church but it'll be empty. I'll walk back out careful to avoid stepping on the skeletons and cross bones on the marble tombs in the floor. In the distance I'll see another poster and a crowd of mourners nearby. I'll follow them until I spot a cat sitting outside a warped old wooden door with a lion and a ring through its nose instead of a door knob. I'll recognize the archway."

"And the devastation," Father adds.

"Yes, everything's the same as in the picture except that I'm in it now. Her feet are all that I can see of her. She faces the archway as if she were trying to run out when the building collapsed and buried her. I begin moving the stones off the mound one by one until she's uncovered. Her extended arm is frozen, burning to reach for something that could save her. Her fingers are perfectly straight as if she were about to touch the lion on the door. She was about to touch her future."

She wipes her eyes. Father holds her hand and encourages her to finish her story.

She nods and continues. "Her skin is smooth and round as if it doesn't bear the weight of the boulders that fell on top of her. On her dress there isn't a single crease, not even where the fullness of her skirt would naturally form pleats. Her nose, the highest point on her reclined body, hasn't a smudge from the powdery mortar between the stones. I look for a line on her ankles separating the part of her body exposed from the part that was buried but there is none. Not even a difference in skin color.

"I get down on my knees beside her and tug at her dress. She doesn't move. I tap her on the knee. She doesn't move. I shake her calf, then shake it again and lean forward to massage the muscle with all the strength in my fingers. I do this again and again and get up and do the same thing to her other leg before I cover her with a blanket.

"Then suddenly, the door flings open. She rises from the dirt floor and walks through the Roman archway. The cat follows behind her. She's too far along before I think to dust off the reddish brown streaks on the back of her dress from lying on the clay earth."

Father slowly pulls the picture of the girl out of Sophia's hands and asks her if she'll have the strength to hold onto to her faith.

"After all," he continues, "it seemed to me that you had doubts about your grandmother's starter dough and were a bit surprised it rose as high as it did."

"Father, I know my sister," I say, putting my arm around her. "She believes the dough can even rise from the dead. After all, she's taking it back to Castroreale with her."

Sophia regains her composure. "It will. Rise," she says with confidence.

When her last word touches the ceiling, it's as though an angel breaks it into a thousand pieces and, like crumbs from the crust of bread, scatters them all over the room.

Roman Arches

A Lucille Ball fan club with thousands of members still meets every year. There's a museum and film festival in her native Jamestown, New York and a tour of the *I Love Lucy* set in Hollywood. My mother hasn't been to any of these, but she's the most devoted fan there is: She thinks she's Lucy Ricardo.

My mother's been Lucy Ricardo off and on for years now, ever since I left the area and moved to Maine. My father died when I was in fifth grade, and the only thing my mother seems to remember now was that she told my dad not to smoke so much because he wouldn't be able to sing "Babalu" if he got throat cancer. This was typical behavior around the Bernardi household, or should I say Ricardo household. My mother seemed to turn Lucy on and off at will, and I knew it was a matter of time before her second personality became a nuisance. That I missed her sixtieth birthday because I had a gallery opening a couple of weeks ago may have put her back on the Lucy track, so I wasn't too surprised the day my mother's parish priest, Father Alfonse, called me and asked if I would come by the rectory as soon as I arrive for my annual Christmas visit. He cited a "family emergency," and hung up the phone without elaborating.

Father Alfonse knows I'm not married. I don't have children or a full-time job. My mother told him I throw pots on a wharf in Maine. Like my mother, I bet he has this image of me hurling a set of Revereware out the window of an old fisherman's shack and into the water, starting with the frying pan and working my way up to the five-quart steamer.

Despite his urgent tone, I'm expecting the usual. My mother probably still hasn't forgiven me that I missed her birthday, but I offered to pay for her to come to Maine and we'd celebrate there. Plus she could come to my opening and be there for my first solo show and jury award.

I realize it's hard to explain to her and Father Alfonse the satisfaction I get from centering clay with my hands as it spins on a potter's wheel that I pump with my bare feet. The resistance I encounter from a lump as it rotates out of kilter because it has to be guided into the middle to its symmetrical peace.

I wish I could tell my mother that I tried but never could learn how to make pottery until I left home. Before I had always ended up with a lopsided mess. The result of sweat on my brow from the clay's push and pull, to shape it against its will. It wasn't art. It was manipulation. I was shaping clay the way priests like Father Alfonse had tried to mold me into a good Catholic girl. I had resisted as much as the clay.

As soon as I walk into his office, Father Alfonse offers me a cup of homemade eggnog, without rum, alas. He doesn't bother with small talk.

"Arabella, your mother is possessed by a red-headed devil, and it'll take a miracle to snap her out of it. As her daughter, I think you should know."

The thought of a red-headed devil makes me snicker but I repress the impulse.

"Father, her Lucy Ricardo routine is just an act. It always has been. I know this time of year you take particular offense to the way she decorates her tree, but forgive me for saying that this is not what I'd call an emergency."

"I grant you, It's bad enough she has figurines of Rock Hudson and Danny Kaye and William Holden in the nativity as the three kings. But this year she . . ."

"Let me guess, she took down the North Star on top of the tree and put up one with a picture of John Wayne on it."

"That's right!" he says in amazement. "As you know from your Catholic upbringing, Arabella, the star symbolizes the way to Bethlehem, not the Hollywood walk of fame."

"I'll see what I can do. At least she's predictable," I reassure him and then grab a slice of nutroll from the coffee table.

"Then you know her feet are purple?" Father asks.

"What are you talking about?"

He leans forward in his chair. "Your mother must miss the old country. She's making her own wine."

"I remember the episode. The one where she goes to Italy and stomps in a vat of grapes to soak up local color?"

"Yes, yes. She won't let anyone wash her feet. Or drain the tub of grape juice. I care about your mother, Arabella, but she is completely *pazz'*. She's even bottling it!"

I choke on my nutroll. "Are you serious?"

"Yes! She insisted I store a jug in the sacristy until midnight Mass on Christmas Eve. She wants me to use it for the consecration!"

"The blood of Christ!" I bounce up from my chair and all the crumbs on my lap fall to the floor. So does the napkin. I hurriedly reach down to pick it up.

"Never mind about that! Go home to your mother. And for the love of God, wash those feet! In the name of the father, the son, and the holy spirit," he says as he makes the sign of the cross.

I thank Father Alfonse and walk to my mother's house a few blocks away, thinking about what he said about my mother's feet. How could that be when she insisted as a child I walk around in orthopedic slippers because she didn't want me tracking in dirt from outside? That went for everyone who set foot in our house. She said we couldn't afford to get a new carpet. She even made us wash our feet along with our hands when I came in with my friends from play-ing. I used to want to catch her with dirty soles so I could order her to the bathroom to wash hers, but they were always so white from the rose powder she sprinkled on after soaking them in a bucket of hot water every night before bed. Nobody missed my mother's "No Shoes" sign taped prominently on the door like a wreath.

When I was a kid, I used to tell her she thought too much about feet, and she said that's because they were our foundations in life and bore the weight of everything we stood on and stood for. She told that to everybody who walked in the door. Even the Fuller Brush man, especially after he complained of a foot cramp while taking off his shoes. When he opened up his black case and reached for one of his brushes, my mother picked up his shoe without flinching at the stench and looked inside.

"A salesman on the circuit wearing these? No wonder! My daugh-ter has better arch support in her slippers!" She dropped his loafer so hard, the penny fell out from its slot. Then she examined his feet and quickly concluded, "Just what I thought. Flat as can be."

The man took out a bigger brush from his suitcase and started to give a sales pitch.

"Enough about bristles," she interrupted. "Why do you think the Romans invented arches? Because someone took the time to look down at their feet and see that they don't just hold up our bodies. They lift us towards the heavens."

The Fuller Brush man gathered up his wares, closed his suitcase, and quickly slipped on his shoes while my mother gave him direc-tions to a five and dime store where he could buy himself a pair. After he left, my mother launched into an old tale about a peasant with fallen arches in her Italian ancestral village.

"His feet were so flat and callused and bubbling with blisters that much of the time he crawled, scraping the earth with his fingers and toes because he was too poor to afford a pair of shoes. The villagers were superstitious and thought the peasant was tied to the under-world and that's why he couldn't stand upright. When they saw him coming, they formed a human chain and blocked off the stone archway leading into town so he couldn't pass under. He hobbled and crawled toward the church. A woman said to him, 'Do you see the dome of our basilica? It is so high it touches the heavens, but it will fall flat on its face like you if we allow you to pass through.'"

I was fourteen and I wanted to go to the movies. "Mom, I'm late . . ."

"Nobody took pity on the peasant man except for a little girl whose father was a cobbler. Digging up one of the man's footprints in a clod of mud, she set the patch of earth on her father's worktable and begged him to make the peasant a pair of leather shoes."

"The cobbler measured the man's foot in the muddy clump and couldn't help but notice there was a solid imprint where his arch should have been. He took a strip of leather hanging on the wall and began cutting and pounding it into shape," my mother said, banging on the door. "When he finished hammering on the sole and punching holes for the laces, he sewed a giant arch inside each shoe."

"With the shoes tied inside a muslin cloth, the girl ran back to the outskirts of town to give them to the peasant. He ran his fingers along the smooth surface and inhaled the musky scent before running into a nearby stream to wash his feet and put on the new shoes."

"Mom, *McCabe and Mrs. Miller* starts in twenty minutes."

"As he stood up," she went on, "the arches lifted him like a springboard. He soared into the sky, disappearing into the clouds. By then the villagers got word of the man's ascent and all eyes were in the heavens. There was nothing to see except white clouds sculpted across the sky like a lace tablecloth until suddenly the clouds dissolved in the sunlight. They spotted the man flying above their basilica as though he were hanging on the cross atop the church dome. The villagers threw themselves to their knees and bowed their heads on the cobblestone. When the peasant landed on the ground, they took turns kissing his feet. A beautiful story, no?"

I was so glad the story was over I could've kissed *her* feet. Instead,

I blew my kisses at Warren Beatty in the movie I saw with my friend Anna Marie.

I wonder if my mother still remembers that story as I slip off my shoes in her doorway. I don't want her to hear so I tiptoe in my bare feet, but it doesn't matter because the TV is so loud. She's in the kitchen, right in the middle of watching *I Love Lucy*, of course.

My mother's an Italian Lucy, all right. Dark skinned, espresso eyes with dyed red hair and roots as black and greasy as oil-cured olives. Her lipstick veers off course the way a car skids off the road. False eyelashes are shadows of her real ones. A short, hourglass figure is exaggerated by a cross-your-heart bra that lifts and separates her breasts like two torpedoes ready to aim and fire. If I didn't know any better, I'd probably duck and cover. Once I graduated from college, my mother began wearing outfits from the 1950s. She went to used clothing stores and bought stuff like a polka-dotted, taffeta dress— the kind that's so full and stiff, it sounds like sandpaper when she walks. She bought a thin sweater with three-quarter-length sleeves she rolled up to her elbows.

When I look at her over the immense plastic leaves in the planter, I can see she's wearing the dress and the sweater. I glance down at her feet. She's wearing heavy knee socks.

"Surprise! I'm home early!" I walk in and give her a big hug.

"Oh! You're here!"

"I stopped at the store and got you a few things."

"Should I put on a pot of coffee?"

We unpack the groceries I brought her, but I can't stop thinking about what her feet look like under those socks. Maybe this time she has gone too far. I always ignored her fantasies in my past visits be-cause it seemed like a harmless act, but now I decide that what I need to do is bring her back to reality every time she goes off to Lucyland.

"I've never seen you wear wool knee socks before—how's your circulation been? Do you want me to get you another sweater or a blanket?"

"If I'm cold I'll get it. What do you think I do when you're not here?"

"I was just offering."

"Please. I'm not a cripple yet."

"I know that. Have you done all your Christmas shopping? I'll take you . . ."

"Whatever I'm going to do is done."

"How about the cookies? I bet the dough's in the freezer ready to go."

"Remember the time I got stuck in the freezer, trying to hide a side of beef from Ricky? I nearly froze to death," she says, handing me the fish sticks I bought her to put in the fridge.

Here we go, I think to myself. Her gestures are now Lucy Ricardo's, not her own. She puts her thumbnail between her front teeth when she looks troubled and lifts her eyebrows when she's got an idea.

"How about the time a loving cup was stuck over my head and I got lost on the subway because I couldn't see where I was going?"

"That was on the New York subway. You live outside of Pittsburgh and take the bus." I decide I've got to see her feet pronto. "What about your feet? Are you keeping them clean like you always have? Let me see."

"I'm making wine like an Italian."

She pulls out the grapes I brought. If only I had talked to Father Alfonse before I went shopping!

"I need to crush some more grapes."

"You're not Lucy, Mom. We can watch reruns anytime you want to."

"You know who gets credit for that, don't you? Desi. Thanks to my husband, you can watch me over and over again. He was so smart to film the show. It came to him like a vision," she says, making the sign of the cross.

"Mom, let me show you something."

I take her to the living room, hoping that the sight of something like our family pictures will bring her back to reality. One glance and

I'm relieved to see it still looks the same. I spot the bulky green sofa I loved when I was little. The tops of the pillows were so wide I could lie on them just like I did on the rear windowsill of our car when we went to the drive-in. The TV set is a tall and skinny box of blonde wood—the same one from my childhood. I'm amazed it's lasted this long. The top half is the tube and the bottom half the scratchy, cloth netting where the sound comes out. I know it's abrasive because I used to put my ear up to it when my mother was in the kitchen.

Glass brandy snifters are dangerously close to the edge of the windowsill. She used to fill them with colored water, but it must have evaporated. She keeps all the windows shut so every surface in the house seems to have grown a layer of crust as if baking in an oven. The air is warm and parched and smells like someone's breath. The lamp with its green frosted globe, which I broke a couple of times playing ball in the living room, is still there but the room is missing a light.

"Where's the lamp I made you?"

My mother sits on the couch and continues her Lucy routine. "Are you accusing me of cheating?"

It's a good thing I've watched all the Lucy episodes with her enough times that I can pick up a cue before I try to make sense of what she's saying. I look down at the living room rug, the same one I learned how to do my first somersault on, which is clearly marked with grape juice stains.

I look up at the photographs on the wall and try another tactic.

"Look at these pictures. There's me. There's Dad and he's with me. You were married to him, not Desi Arnaz."

She doesn't budge from the corner of the couch, so I sit down on the couch next to her and tuck my legs inside the crack between the pillows the way I did when I was little, waiting for her to do the same. This is what we did when we watched *Lucy* together. When she was my mother, not Lucy Ricardo.

I pat the pillow. "You and I watched *Lucy* every day right here before lunch. Do you remember how you strained out the celery in my pastina because I didn't like it. And picked off the parsley in the meatballs. And how about the sandwiches you made me? You trimmed the crust off Zia's homemade Italian bread. That was me? Remember? Rose's daughter, Arabella."

I reach for her hand and wait for the Italian in her to reply. It works as she grunts, "Who ever heard of an Italian who doesn't like breadcrust? If my aunt saw what I did to a loaf of her bread, she would have . . . I don't even want to think what she would have done. The things I did to get you to eat." She was herself again. Now if I could just get a look at her feet.

"How long are you here for, anyway?" she asks abruptly.

"I want to be home for New Year's Eve so we can have the whole week together."

She stares at the crack between the couch pillows before bouncing up to run to the closet. Tossing off the lid of a shoebox, she puts on the red velvet hat she finds there. Then she reaches in the same box for a bottle of Pepto-Bismol and a spoon and begins reciting lines from an episode where Lucy rehearses a TV commercial for alcohol-laced "Vitametavegamin." Each time she swallows a teaspoon, Mom/Lucy slurs her words.

"Are you unpoopular? Do you pop out at parties?"

"No more Lucy, Mom. Please! I came home to see you for Christmas. All those years you made seven-fish stew on Christmas Eve and you let me stir with the wooden spoon. And how you hung stockings for La Befana to fill on Epiphany. I loved that we celebrated the twelve days of Christmas. Remember I rolled off my twin bed in the middle of the night before Christmas one year? You and Dad were up late wrapping presents and heard the thud of me hitting the hardwood floor. You pulled out every single pin curl to feel for lumps on my head. You didn't care what my hair looked like for church on Christmas day. And when I couldn't fall back asleep, you said to lie on my back and draw a picture of Babbo Natale on the ceiling. I was so glad you said that and not to close my eyes and pray. When you even promised me one of your brandy plums! You told me that. Not

Lucy Ricardo." I hug my mother and add, "That was your specialty. Not stomping grapes in the bathtub."

Suddenly, my mother darts toward the bathroom. I cut her off. "Where are you going!"

When I get to the bathroom, I find the tub is filled with a vinegary mush. Red grapes, white grapes, yellow grapes. Squashed and fermenting.

"I don't believe this mess! And you tracked it around the house! Mom, we need to clean this up and your feet right now. Let's start by taking those socks off."

She doesn't move from the doorway.

"Then sit on the toilet and I'll help you."

She sits but won't help with the socks. After a struggle, I yank one off. Her foot is so stained that I would barely make out her toes if it weren't for all the seeds in the cracks between them. So neglected that I can't stand to look at them. Father Alfonse wasn't exaggerating. Maybe she is *pazz':* crazy. I fill a bucket of water and set it by the toilet.

"I'm doing this for the church you know."

"So I hear. Take that other sock off and step in this. Your feet don't look like they've been washed in months. We're going to get them clean so you can put on your orthopedic slippers."

"I threw them out."

"Why?"

"Because the closer your feet are to the ground, the easier it is to smash the grapes."

Her feet are now submerged in the bucket. I let go of her ankles to get the brush. She waits until I'm poking in the cabinet under the sink to make her move.

"Watch me! I'm turning water into wine," she shrieks, stomping back and forth in the tub.

"Mom! You're going to slip and fall."

"No," she shouts back. "*Lucy* reruns are the only way you'll come and see me."

"Is that what this is about?! Let me help you!"

By the time I grab her arm, my mother's feet are two sinking ships in a sea of skins, juice, and seeds and she is getting more feisty.

"You want to help? Then come on in! Come on!"

I won't go in with her because I remember in the episode, Lucy fights with an Italian woman in the grape vat. I try to be reasonable. "I know what you're up to. That's not the kind of help I'm talking about."

"Get in here and get to work crushing grapes!"

"Mom, please . . ."

"Help your mother!"

"You won't let me! Now come out or I'm going to have to drag you out of this tub! Do you hear me?!"

Just as I had feared, my mother follows the *Lucy* episode to its climax. She hurls a handful of grapes at me to start a fight and slips and falls in the process, taking me down with her. I had never heard my mother scream in as much pain as she did at that moment.

Wearing a purple stain on the entire left side of my shirt and pants, I rush my mother to the emergency room. Not because she's Lucy Ricardo, but because she's broken her foot.

As soon as she sees the doctor, she asks how long the operation will be. He mumbles something about the bone being shattered, but my mother is disoriented and confused from the painkillers. I tell her anywhere from four to six *I Love Lucy* episodes. She's in so much pain, she doesn't even move to put her thumbnail between her front teeth so I know the drugs aren't working yet.

Mom hasn't said a word to me since we landed in the tub together. When the doctor leaves the room, I remind her of the episode where Lucy takes up sculpting in the hopes she'll talk again or just get her mind off the pain.

"What was it like for you to shape clay with your hands? I bet it wasn't easy to have Fred as a model?"

She doesn't answer me and then two nurses come in and wheel her to surgery, leaving me alone in the waiting room. Hours go by and I grow tired. I try to rest my eyes but I think I see two orderlies in white wheel a stretcher down the hall with a sheet covering a form. Even though I know she only broke her foot, I suddenly see my mother's corpse in my minds eye and I want to look under the sheet to see if my mother is there, but the body is quickly pushed onto an elevator. I follow the numbers as they light up . . . 6, 7, 8, 9, 10. There's a pause at 10, and then the lights go down to 5. The two orderlies wheel a cart off the elevator. It's the same corpse as before. I know because I memorized the creases in the sheets the way someone can recall the wrinkles in a lover's face, the worry lines above the forehead, the smile lines around the mouth, the lines surrounding the eyes that map out contemplation.

Now I'm convinced it's my mother. I rush to the cart but a white glove stops me from getting any closer. The orderlies wheel her out and let a couple dressed in black inside before reentering the elevator. This time they go down . . . 5, 4, 3, 2, 1, G, B. They've taken her to the basement. I press the button but the elevator never comes. I run to the stairs only to find the door's locked.

Suddenly, I hear a big thud and turn to see a box falling from the ceiling onto the round coffee table back in the waiting room. When the box lands, a big lump of clay falls out and rests on the center of the table. I sit down and twirl the table until it spins on its own. I fill a washbasin from a storage room with warm water and splash the clay with a damp washcloth. My fingers glide along the clay's smoothness until I feel muscles twitching inside. A woman's feet take shape effortlessly on my fingertips. They are long and slender, the heels narrow. The arches are strikingly curved, and they are as smooth as the inside of a seashell. I finish dabbing them with a washcloth and then pat them dry. They are my mother's feet, the most beautiful creation I've ever made.

I awake to a nurse who says I can see my mother now. The doctor is waiting for me in her room and tells me that the operation was successful but that it is going to take some time for her to recover. She's very weak and groggy at the moment, although I can wake her up if I wish. But I'm worried because I don't know if she'll be Lucy Ricardo or my mother. Asleep, she's my mother. Her dyed hair is covered in a cap. Her fake eyelashes, which always made me think I was seeing double, are gone. Her lips are silent and still. The animation is gone. No gestures at all, just the simple movement of her white cotton gown puffing in and out with her chest. I lift up the sheet to look down at her feet. The one that isn't in a cast is still dirty so I wipe it with a washcloth and warm water until the stains are gone. Hers and mine.

As I pat it dry, I want to call her name but don't know which one to use. I hold back what comes naturally and think of what my mother would prefer.

"Lucy," I say in a whisper. "Lucy, you have company." In a sing-song fashion, I pull the line Ricky once said.

She doesn't awaken.

"Lucy?" I get a little closer and whisper. Looking down at her, I know I'd rather have what little is left of my mother than all of Lucy. I speak louder. "Are you ready to go home? I'm going to take care of you now. It's me, Arabella. Mom?"

She slowly opens her eyes. It's as though shades are drawn, and a big picture window allows me to see my mother for the first time.

Curt Leviant
Ladies and Gentlemen, The Original Music of the Hebrew Alphabet *and*
    Weekend in Mustara: *Two Novellas*

David Milofsky
A Friend of Kissinger: A Novel

Lesléa Newman
A Letter to Harvey Milk: Short Stories

Ladette Randolph
This Is Not the Tropics: Stories

Sara Rath
The Star Lake Saloon and Housekeeping Cottages: A Novel

Mordecai Roshwald
Level 7

Lewis Weinstein
The Heretic: A Novel